STUCK ON EARTH

DAVID KLASS

FRANCES FOSTER BOOKS
Farrar Straus Giroux
New York

Distributed in Canada by D&M Publishers, Inc.
Printed in February 2010 in the United States of America
by RR Donnelley & Sons Company, Harrisonburg, Virginia
Designed by Jay Colvin
First edition, 2010
1   3   5   7   9   10   8   6   4   2

www.fsgkidsbooks.com

Library of Congress Cataloging-in-Publication Data
Klass, David.
    Stuck on Earth / David Klass.— 1st ed.
        p.   cm.
    Summary: On a secret mission to evaluate whether the human race
should be annihilated, a space alien inhabits the body of a bullied
fourteen-year-old boy.
    ISBN: 978-0-374-39951-1
    [1. Extraterrestrial beings—Fiction.   2. Bullying—Fiction.   3. Science
fiction.]   I. Title.

PZ7.K67813St 2010
[Fic]—dc22

                                                                    2008048133

For Anatol

STUCK ON EARTH

1

We are skimming over the New Jersey countryside in full search mode, hunting a fourteen-year-old. Our shields are up, and no humans can possibly spot us, even with the aid of their primitive "radar" and "sonar" technologies.

Earth's lone moon is in the sky above us. This is indeed a pretty planet. I can see why the Lugonians, whose sun is about to supernova, covet it. Beneath us are dwelling places known as "houses" separated by expanses of unused space termed "lawns" that convey status on property owners by showing how much land they can afford to waste.

A target subject has just been identified! The circumstances are favorable for an extraction—he is sitting alone eating a "snack"—an unnecessary meal that is known to be unhealthy and is consumed at odd hours. It falls under the category of addictive behavior that most Homo sapiens find impossible to resist.

Cellular spectroscopy is positive. This specimen is

Caucasian, fourteen years old, and in good health. Weak areas appear to be the teeth, where a metallic correction device known as "braces" has been fastened, and the eyes, where ocular aids called "glasses" have been appended with the help of two plastic rods hooked around the ears.

Brain scans show an above average human intelligence quotient, with particularly high cognitive and imaginative ability. A probe of long-term memory reveals that the specimen is named Tom Filber, he lives with his parents in a small house on Beech Avenue, and he has a sister named Sally with whom he is in a constant state of conflict that sometimes escalates into violence.

All systems are go! The Preceptor Supervisor has just approved the extraction. I, Ketchvar III, prepare myself to inhabit the body and mind of an infinitely lower life-form. I remind myself that my mission is vitally necessary—we must decide soon if the human species should be preserved or wiped out. We drop low in our ship till we are hovering above the chimney of 330 Beech Avenue.

We have just established direct visual surveillance of the specimen. He is sitting on his front porch, devouring large flakes of dehydrated potato, drained of all nutritional value and flavored with artificial taste stimulants. Every now and then he apparently finds a flake not to his liking, spits it to the floor, and crushes it under the heel of his boot.

Our Mission Engineer readies the paralysis ray. We all turn toward our Preceptor Supervisor, who gives the go-ahead.

The ray is turned on. Specimen Filber freezes in mid-chew. Sensors show a wild spike in his adrenaline and a rapid acceleration of his heartbeat—he knows something is happening to him, but he cannot make a sound or move a muscle.

Antigravity suction commences immediately. He is lifted off the porch and drawn into the cargo bay of our spaceship. The specimen still cannot move or speak, but he stares back at us through his ocular aids with big, brown, frightened human eyes.

2

"Do not be alarmed, Earthling," I say, crawling out of my protective shell. Homo sapiens are large and ugly creatures, but I try not to show distaste. I remind myself that to this human I must resemble the Earth organism known as a snail.

Tom Filber cannot move a muscle. Even the pupils of his eyes cannot dilate. Still, the human face is extremely expressive and his terror shows clearly. The paralysis ray did not freeze his major internal organs, and his heart rate continues to climb precipitously. I'm afraid he may undergo cardiac arrest if I do not find a way to calm his fears.

"Hello, Tom. You don't mind if I call you that, do you? My name is Ketchvar. Please try to relax. Would you like a sip of water?"

I modify the paralysis ray to return control of his vocal cords, larynx, and the other bodily parts required for speech.

Tom Filber slowly opens his mouth and licks his lips.

"Please don't eat me," he whispers. "I have a rash and it's highly contagious, so if you eat me you'll catch it and die."

"I have no plans to ingest you," I tell him. I try to recall some other typical human fears about extraterrestrials and attempt to set his mind at ease. "Nor am I interested in dissecting you to learn about human anatomy. And here's some more good news, Tom—I also do not intend to try to impregnate you."

My reassurances do not have the intended soothing effect. His blood pressure surges and he begins hyperventilating. He moistens his lips with his tongue again and whispers, "Take my sister."

Human thought processes are notoriously difficult to follow. "Take her for what?" I ask.

"For whatever," he says. "She's fatter than I am so she's probably more delicious to eat. And she's a girl so she can have your babies. And she gets A's in school so if you want to dissect a human brain, hers would be much better than mine. That's her window, right there. She's alone, practicing her cello. Take her, and put me back. I swear I won't tell anyone."

"You were chosen because you're the perfect age," I tell him. "We need a fourteen-year-old. It is, in a way, a great honor."

"The perfect age for what?" he whispers suspiciously, watching me slither toward him.

"It won't hurt," I promise him. "It will all be over in a second."

"What won't hurt? What are you going to do?"

"Nothing terrible, so try to stay calm," I assure him, climbing up his leg. "I'm just going to slither through your nostril, crawl into your cranium, and take possession of your brain."

"No!" he says, pleading desperately. "Not my brain! Anything but that!" Somehow, despite the biomagnetic grip of the paralysis ray, a tear squeezes out of his right eye and runs down his cheek. "I promise I'll be good. I'll do my homework and brush my teeth and pray to God and be nice to Sally and eat less sweets and make my bed and . . ."

I have reached his hip. "None of that is necessary," I tell him. "Please don't change on my account, Tom Filber. I need you to stay just the way you are. You're going to help me. We're going to work together."

The human abruptly stops begging and making promises, and his whisper hardens. "Listen, you little piece of Martian snot. Get down from me right now and I might let you slime away and live. I won't step on you or drop you in salt water. You crawl up one inch higher, just one more inch, and I swear to God I'll squash you like a potato chip! Not one more inch. I'M WARNING YOU!"

I crawl up his shoulder to his neck.

He begins to heave in great gasps of air. "Okay, look, let's make a deal. You're in luck. I know where it is."

"Where what is?" I ask, baffled.

"Whatever you're after," he gasps quickly. "The key. The formula. The stuff. I know where they've hidden it. I can get it for you. You think I won't because I love the human race? Hah! I hate them all. I have more in common with

8

you. Let's work together. Tell me what you want and I'll get it. We'll split the take. Fifty-fifty. Deal?"

I reach his chin.

"Did I say fifty-fifty? I mean sixty-forty. Seventy-thirty. Oh, GOD, STOP! GOD, GOD, GOD! Oh, GOD. MOMMY!"

He is truly in danger of a life-threatening coronary event. There is no time to lose.

I take a breath and go in through the left nasal passage. It is dark and slimy so I don't waste time. Right turn, left turn, squeeze through, crawl around, slither over, and there it is! The human brain—the organ that has made these furless warm-blooded bipeds the laughingstock of the universe. I enfold it, and using the Thromborg Technique, I infuse myself into it and become Tom Filber.

3

I, Ketchvar III, am a Sandovinian, from the planet Sandoval IV. Our bodies are small and weak, and we spend
our lives in protective shells, relying on robots to accomplish even the simplest tasks.

Tom Filber's body feels terribly exposed, but it is also
strangely liberating to have eyes, ears, nose, and skin exposed to the open air. This big, bony body is a giant new
machine, and it takes me a few minutes to get the hang of
it. I lurch around the spaceship, fall down on my rear end,
and get back up.

But I don't have long to practice walking. Once an
extraction has been performed, the insertion must take
place almost immediately or the risk that the specimen's
absence will be discovered by his fellow humans increases
exponentially.

In this case, I see that Mrs. Filber has walked onto the
porch and is sweeping up the chips and shouting, "Tom,
where are you? I warned you if you left chips on the floor

again I'd fix your wagon! You made this mess so come and pay the piper!" She is a big woman, and her voice is getting louder by the moment. "DON'T MAKE ME FIND YOU, TOM, OR YOU'LL REGRET IT!"

Why Tom's mother would want to fix a wagon because he spilled chips on the floor is not clear, nor do I understand why a piper needs to be paid. But there's clearly no time to lose. I must descend to 330 Beech Avenue and insert myself into human society right away. However, one final task must be attended to.

Tom Filber's consciousness was displaced during the Thromborg Technique. Now I must lock it into a Ragwellian Bubble and suspend it inside his parietal lobe. When my mission is finished and I am ready to relinquish control of this body, I will restore Tom's consciousness to its rightful place. Till then, his essence will float, observing everything that happens through the window of the bubble but incapable of resisting or taking any willful actions. I will be able to access his consciousness when I require human expertise on how to deal with a situation that exceeds my ability to understand or improvise.

Tom Filber does not go easily into the bubble. His consciousness and will are surprisingly strong for such a primitive life-form. Meanwhile, Mrs. Filber is getting so loud that someone in a nearby house shouts for her to put a lid on it. Clearly, the time element is critical. I force Tom into the bubble, lock it up, and reverse the antigravity suction.

Out the cargo bay door I float, down to the darkest

patch of lawn on the side of Tom's porch. No one sees me descend to Earth.

I land on a carpet of grass. I see right away that I was wrong about the reason for these lawns. They are not merely status symbols. They have an unexpected pleasantness to them—a soft, embracing feel and a sweet smell. Also, the lawn and the old crab apple tree growing out of it provide some sense of separation from the neighboring house at 332 Beech Avenue.

This separation is apparently not sufficient, because as I walk quickly toward the porch I hear Mrs. Filber—whom I shall hereafter refer to as my mother—shout out, "Tom, don't make me count! I'm warning you for the last time. ALL RIGHT, I'M COUNTING! TEN, NINE, EIGHT . . ."

And a male voice from the window of 332 Beech Avenue calls out: "RUTH FILBER, ARE YOU LAUNCHING A ROCKET OUT THERE? PUT A LID ON IT OR I'M GOING TO CALL THE COPS!"

My mother breaks off from her countdown to respond: "GO AHEAD AND CALL THEM. I'D HAVE SOME THINGS TO TELL THEM ABOUT THE GOINGS-ON AT YOUR PLACE, WOULDN'T I? LEAVING CHILDREN UNSUPERVISED ALL NIGHT. SEVEN, SIX, FIVE."

"I work nights. What else can I do?" the voice from the window replies in a more reasonable tone.

"YOU CAN DO JUST WHAT I'M DOING NOW, AND TAKE RESPONSIBILITY FOR YOUR KIDS!"

my mother shouts back. "Now, do you have anything else to say to me right now, or can I discipline my son in peace?"

The window slams shut, and my mother says, "Tom, I'm at five seconds. FOUR. THREE . . ."

I can see her clearly now. Standing atop the porch steps, backlit by the fluorescent bulb, she looks enormous. She is holding a broom in her hands like some sort of fearsome cudgel, and I hesitate a second more.

"TWO!" she calls out. "TOM, I SAID TWO! NEXT COMES ONE. THIS IS YOUR VERY LAST WARNING. I'LL GROUND YOU FOR A MONTH. YOU'LL LOSE ALL COMPUTER AND TV PRIVILEGES. YOU'LL HAVE TO MAKE YOUR SISTER'S BED. TWO FOR THE LAST TIME. OKAY, ONE. GOING ONCE. GOING TWICE . . ."

I walk out of the darkness into the light, open my mouth, and speak with a human voice for the very first time: "Good evening, Mother. You're looking quite well. I was just out for a brief constitutional."

She looks back at me, mouth agape. "Brief what?"

"Constitutional," I repeat, giving her one of those "smiles" that Earthlings apparently find calming. "A walk taken regularly for one's health. Is it not a lovely evening?"

"I'm going to give *you* a constitutional," she announces, "right in the backside." She descends the stairs, broom in hand. No doubt if she knew the fate of the human race might be forever sealed by her violent behavior she would act with more restraint. But I can't tell her that.

Nor do I want to get hit by her broom. I quickly access

the consciousness of Tom Filber in the Ragwellian Bubble.

Will she really hit me or is she bluffing?

Are you kidding? She'll swat you the first chance she gets.

Does it hurt?

Like hell.

Is that a lot?

Damn straight.

She has reached the bottom of the stairs and is advancing on me, broom held at the ready.

What should I do?

Duck behind the tree and then make a run for it.

I run behind the tree. A squirrel squints down at me from a high branch. This is a medium-size rodent of the family Sciuridae, and I would enjoy examining it further. Unfortunately, I am being pursued around the tree trunk by my mother who is swinging her broom at me.

"Don't you think I have better things to do than clean up your messes!" she demands furiously. "What were you doing out here anyway? Were you sneaking a cigarette? Let me smell your breath. Were you looking up into Michelle Peabody's window? Ha, got you!"

She pretends to circle the tree one way, then quickly darts back the other. I believe this is what humans call a feint. She executes the maneuver with surprising deftness for a woman of her size and bulk.

The broom makes solid contact with my backside. I have never been violently attacked by another life-form in over two thousand years of life. The pain from the blow is bad enough, but the anger behind it and the indignity of being treated this way are even worse.

I am tempted to abort my mission, beam myself back to the ship, and tell the Preceptor to eliminate the entire species. But Homo sapiens deserve a fair chance, even if things are not starting out promisingly. So I take Tom Filber's suggestion and make a run for it, dodging around her follow-up swing and heading straight for the house.

4

Up the stairs I go, onto the porch and into the house with my mother in full pursuit. "Where do you think you're going? Clean up that mess on the porch. Did you do your homework? Tom Filber, STOP RIGHT NOW!"

I climb the steep steps to the second floor, guessing that she won't chase me. She makes it up a few steps and slows, breathing hard.

I reach the second floor and duck into the first door I come to. I pull it closed and lock it. Ah, the joy of a safe hiding place! I turn and see a plump girl with a glum expression sitting on a chair drawing a bow back and forth across a cello as if trying to saw it in half.

"Greetings, sister," I say. "I come in peace."

She lowers the bow and stares at me for a moment. "Who invited you in my room, metal mouth?"

"No one," I admit. "How lovely you play."

"What?"

"The cello. How lovely you play the cello. Your approach, while lacking in any appreciable musical quality, is nonetheless characterized by impressive energy."

"Have you lost your mind?" She gets up and fumbles for something on her desk.

"No, I have not lost it," I tell her, "but it's kind of you to ask."

She stares back at me suspiciously. "What's up with you, geekhead? What are you trying to pull?"

"I have not come to pull anything," I assure her. "I will not pull your hair, or your ears, or even one of your little fingers."

"Are you threatening me?" She begins furiously rooting around in her desk, searching for something.

"No, I would be in favor of a complete cessation of hostilities," I tell her. "Let us live in harmony, like the moss and the lichen."

She's found what she's looking for. I see a black bag marked Rape Defense Kit. "I've got some harmony for you here, little brother," she says. "This thing has ten thousand volts and it will fry your eyeballs." She raises what I believe to be an electric cattle prod, switches it on, and walks toward me.

I do not wish to have my eyeballs fried. I turn to the door, but just then I hear a loud knocking. It's my mother. "SALLY, IS YOUR BROTHER HIDING IN THERE? Is he distracting you from your cello practice? Let me in and I'll show him what's what." She shakes the door so hard it looks like it might fly off its hinges.

I'm cornered. There's only one thing to do. I quickly

access the mind of Tom Filber in the Ragwellian Bubble. *Go out the window,* he advises. *There's a tree branch you can grab onto. Head up.*

Sally swipes at me with the cattle prod. It's making a sizzling sound and she's afraid of it herself, so she's holding it far out, away from her body.

I duck around it and bolt for the open window. She comes after me, but I push her cello case at her and she trips on it. By the time she stands back up, I've wiggled my upper body out of the window and grabbed a tree branch.

I see that there are few branches beneath me, and it's a long drop to the ground. So I take Tom's advice and start climbing.

5

I have never climbed a tree before. It's quite difficult, especially in darkness. Luckily there are many small and large branches, and I manage to pull myself up.

I hear voices beneath me. My mother and sister are peering out the window, but they're looking down.

"I think I saw him drop to the ground," Sally says. "He must have run off."

"He'll be back soon," my mother responds. "It's going to be a cold night. He'll freeze his little tootsie off."

I'm not sure what part of the human anatomy she's referring to, but the evening has indeed grown chilly. I hang there for a moment, looking up at the night sky.

The moon is large and luminous—I believe I can make out the outlines of the Sea of Tranquillity. How welcome a bit of tranquillity would be right now! Beyond that luminous moon are the stars of the galaxy, with thousands of peaceful and civilized members of the Galactic Confederation orbiting them. The sun of my own world, Sandoval IV, is a faint pinprick in the Belt of Orion. I close my eyes and imagine the red oozing mud of home, the safety and orderliness of a planet where cruelty and violence have been unknown for two million years.

And then I open my eyes. My sister has begun playing her cello again, and the dissonant chords seem a fitting musical backdrop to this confused and brutal world. Ah, Planet Earth, so beautiful, and in the hands of such buffoons! Perhaps it would be kinder to put species Homo sapiens out of its misery once and for all. But I have just arrived, and it would be irresponsible to make that decision quite yet.

So I follow Tom Filber's instructions and head upward, and soon see an attic with a light on. There is a balcony, and I kick and pull my way up to it and clamber over the lip. Sliding glass doors lead into some sort of small office.

I peer in and see a man sitting in a swivel chair, facing a television set, watching what is known as a reality TV show. We observed this puzzling cultural phenomenon during orbital monitoring. Human beings have brief life spans, and even our top behavioral experts cannot figure out why they regularly give up huge chunks of time to watch other people's supposed real lives.

The man in the chair sits with his eyes riveted on the screen. This must be my father. I slip in when he has his back to me, and step to a shadowy corner to assess the situation.

He has a glass in his hand and is sipping an intoxicant made from barley, known as whiskey. Alcohol is a stimulant, and drinking it often has the effect of making humans violent. Given the tempers of the other members of the Filber family, I fear the worst. Still, the Preceptors have charged me with a vital mission and I must be brave.

"Dad?" I query in a whisper.

His shoulders snap up in surprise and he almost drops his glass. He's a tall, skinny man with a mustache. "What? Who's that?" he shouts, spinning around on his swivel chair.

"Dad, it's me. Tom. Your son."

"How the devil did you get in here? The door's locked."

"I climbed the tree to the balcony. Sally was after me with a cattle prod. And Mom was hitting me with a broom."

He looks back at me, and for a moment I see genuine sympathy in his face. "She loves you very much, son. It's me she wants to be hitting." Then his eyes slowly swing back to the TV screen, as if drawn by magnetic attraction. "Come, sit down and watch this show with me. We'll have a few laughs. It will help you relax. Puts my brain right to sleep. Look at these fools." On the TV, one young woman has just pushed another into a swimming pool.

"Why do you want your brain to go to sleep?" I ask, sitting down near him.

He takes a sip of whiskey and nods. "Sad state of affairs, eh? I know I should be setting a better example." He sees something on the TV that makes him slap his knee. "Look at that. Right into the pool again."

I glance at the screen and then back at him and feel a little sorry for this man who is trying to dull his thought processes. "You don't have to apologize to me," I say. "The life of an Earthling is notoriously unpredictable."

"Very true, son," he agrees. "But why put it that way? You're an earthling yourself, last time I looked." He reluctantly turns away from the TV screen and looks right at me. He has a penetrating stare, but of course he can't tell that I am a space alien from Sandoval who has fused with his son's brain. "Why set yourself apart?"

I meet his gaze. "I don't feel like my usual self tonight."

My father's face must once have been quite handsome. Now it's lined with worry and pain, and his hair is thinning and turning gray. "Let's be honest for a second, Tom. I see what's happening around here and it tears me up. I wish I could help, but I don't know what I can do. Except to tell you that I love you and I'm truly sorry."

On Planet Sandoval, we rarely discuss our feelings openly. In more than two thousand years, my father, Ketchvar II, has never told me that he loves me. The deep bond exists, and it does not need to be spoken of. I am not prepared for this level of emotional intensity on my first evening on Earth. "Everything's okay," I mutter. "I was eating potato chips on the porch, so Mom got angry and . . ."

"Nothing's okay," he interrupts. His voice drops lower. "I know you blame me. You think I married a monster, and you have to put up with Godzilla for a mother. And you're right—fire does come out of her mouth pretty often these days." A thought occurs to him and he asks quickly: "She didn't see that you were heading up here?"

"No, she thinks I climbed down the tree and ran off."

He nods, relieved, and pours himself another glass. "It wasn't always like this." He closes his eyes and spins around in his chair. "She was a sweet woman once."

"Why is she so angry now?" I ask.

"Bitter," he corrects me. "Who can blame her? She had a lot of dreams and not many of them came true. So she vents. And that sister of yours! Not a kind word comes from her mouth from winter to spring." He stops spinning, and opens his eyes. "And look at you, standing there, skinny as a beanpole, halfway to manhood and not a clue."

"Don't worry about me," I tell him. I think to myself: Your compassion is appreciated but misplaced. I will return to Sandoval at light speed when my mission is completed. You are stuck here, married to Godzilla.

He reaches out a long arm. His fingers touch the side of my face. Human skin is extremely sensitive, and I can almost feel an electrical charge. "Blame me if you want, son, but try to enjoy being fourteen. It's a glorious thing to be young and carefree, and it goes by quickly."

"Yes, the human life span is indeed a brief one," I whisper back. "There are Earth organisms like sequoias and bristlecone pines that live twenty times longer."

He stares back at me, and then his hand drops away. "I'm sorry, son. All I can say is it could have worked out very differently! I had my chance and it was a fine one. If only Stan Harbishaw hadn't robbed me blind. Let him keep his factory and rot in hell for it!"

"Who's Stan Harbishaw?"

"The Devil!" he says, and coughs into his palm.

"Dad, maybe you should stop drinking, turn off the TV, and go to bed."

For a split second anger flashes in his face. "You talk to your father that way?"

I back up, wondering if I'll have to make another escape to the high branches, but he heaves a sigh. "No need for the tree again, Tom. Down the steps to your room. Quietly, softly. They won't bother you. Lock yourself in. That's all we can do now. Lock ourselves in and wait for Judgment Day."

He spins away, back to the TV, and takes another drink. His eyes focus on the screen and someone else's supposedly real life. Soon he is completely lost in his show.

I unlock the door and creep out of the attic.

6

To: reveredelders@galacticconfederation.com
Subject: Old Hip-Hop Songs That Sucked

Revered Galactic Confederation Elders, I write this from Tom
Filber's bedroom, at midnight. He has what is known as a "laptop computer," a primitive but functional device, and I am en-
crypting this entry and uploading it to a link our spaceship will
be able to scan. In case the communication is intercepted, I am
assigning it the code name "Old Hip-Hop Songs That Sucked."
My research shows that no Earthling will be remotely interested in trying to unscramble a coded file with such a name.

Esteemed Preceptors, let me begin by thanking you again for
the honor of being chosen for this mission. It is a weighty
responsibility to decide the fate of 6.8 billion life-forms.

In case I am discovered in the act of writing this, I am simul-
taneously pretending to play a computer game that Tom Fil-

ber enjoys. It is, believe it or not, called Galactic Warrior and portrays the human race flying off on spaceships with laser weapons to subdue inferior, threatening, and hideous-looking life-forms. Tom apparently plays this game for several hours every day, and even with my inestimably superior intelligence, I cannot yet match his record point total.

Tom Filber's room is small, with posters of musical entertainers and professional wrestlers decorating the walls. The one tiny window looks across a tangle of branches at a house that belongs to the Peabody family.

Tom is apparently attracted to a young female member of that family named Michelle. Human hormones exert a powerful effect as youths of the species approach mating age. They have invented a complicated construct called "romantic love" to explain and control these primitive urges.

As long as I inhabit Tom's body, I will be subject to all of his strengths and weaknesses, including his chemical impulses. Of course, given my advanced GC training, I can easily control the effects of such a simplistic chemical as testosterone. Nevertheless, as I write this I find I have glanced several times toward the Peabody house, where a light is on in the third-floor window and a female form appears to be moving around behind some drapes.

Now, on to business. I would like to thank Mission Engineers for all their hard work. The extraction and insertion were a complete success. I have been accepted as Tom Filber and have made the acquaintance of every member of his immediate family.

The Filbers are violent and unhappy, perhaps representative of the entire species. My first impressions confirm GC conclusions dating back three thousand years that the human race must never be told of the existence of the Confederation. Their limited intelligence, extreme egotism, xenophobia, and bellicose nature make any such direct contact impossible. Humans simply could not handle the information that they are a small and unimpressive race, nor do they have the wisdom and humility to accept our guidance.

My initial research also tends to confirm projections that their cruelty and violent tendencies will lead them to destroy themselves. I am now using Tom Filber's computer to scan what they call the Internet, a vast garbage can of human knowledge. It is clear that the end point is not far off. I would conservatively estimate it at ten years.

They are within a decade of permanently wrecking their magnificent global environment. Their brightest scientists are laying the groundwork for new and devastating nuclear and biological weapons. GC ethicists may be right that we owe it to weak and vulnerable Homo sapiens to euthanize the species quickly and painlessly before such nightmares are unleashed.

Of course, the Lugonians would then be free to take possession of this planet as their own. The Lugonian emissaries are probably correct—this may indeed be the best course for all concerned. But I will not prejudge. Tomorrow should provide me with crucial information.

During our extensive orbital monitoring, we observed that nearly all of the bad habits manifested by adult humans can be traced back to their early development and were acquired and reinforced during a twelve-year period of voluntary daily incarceration known as "school."

We further discovered that the preponderance of destructive behavior, illogical thinking, and counterproductive tendencies develop in Homo sapiens during their fourteenth year, when their bodies hit a growth spurt, their hormones flare, and their voluntary incarceration reaches the highest stress level as they become "freshmen" in "high school."

Tomorrow I will experience this for myself.

I will be going to high school as a freshman!

Signing off now. Your humble evaluator, Ketchvar III.

7

At first I think they are saying, "Ask him." It is hard to make out the words clearly because it is a windy day and they are hissing at me from across the street. I hear it faintly as I walk up Maple Drive with my backpack bouncing with every step. "Ask him," they hiss.

I smile and remain calm. "Ask who?" I call back. "And when I find out who he is, what should I inquire?"

Then it's "Ass slim." Many of them are younger kids on their way to the elementary or middle schools, which are nearby. I have no idea why they are following me. They are making me self-conscious. We have observed young Earthlings extensively from orbit, so I know I am correctly groomed and attired. I have chosen blue jeans and a flannel shirt from the selection in Tom Filber's closet. They laugh and call out to me, and the howling wind swallows their words: "Ass slim. Ass slim."

"No slimmer than the norm," I tell them. "Perhaps you mean it as a compliment. Thank you. It's kind of you to pay such attention to the contours of my buttocks. But let us focus on other things. Is it not a lovely, blustery morning? I can smell the late-flowering hibiscus."

My words only whip them up to a greater level of excitement. They laugh and shriek. "Did you hear that? The contours of his buttocks! Late-flowering hibiscus! He's so weird! Ass slim, ass slim."

It's only when we leave the road and cut across a leafy shortcut that the wind dies down and I hear it clearly. One boy—he can't be more than ten years old—runs very close to me, opens his mouth wide, and yells out "HEY, ALIEN!"

I freeze, terrified. Can all my advanced GC training have been for nothing? Has my insertion been discovered already? What possibly could have tipped them off? I am, after all, inhabiting a human body, dressed and behaving appropriately, and consulting with Tom Filber's consciousness when necessary.

"LET'S SEE IF YOUR BLOOD IS GREEN, ALIEN!" the boy shouts, and throws a stick at me.

I dodge and it misses me. "My blood is red," I tell him, "as is true of all mammals. Please leave me alone."

A bigger kid hurries over. Based on their facial resemblance, I guess that he is the older brother of the boy who hurled the stick. He has hit his growth spurt and stands nearly six feet tall. Muscles ripple on his arms. "Who gave you permission to speak to my bro, Alien?"

I look back at him. "I meant no harm. Why do you call me that?"

"Because it's your name, you freak show. Always has

been. Always will be. Do you have a problem with that?"

I realize the remarkable truth. I have randomly appropriated the body of an outsider, a boy who never fit in and was nicknamed Alien by the other children of the neighborhood! This must be why Tom Filber claimed in the spaceship that he had things in common with me. Perhaps this coincidence will make my masquerade on Earth much easier. "Yes, I am an alien," I say. "You're right, I always have been. I have no problem with admitting that."

"Get him, Scott!" other kids encourage. "Git the alien! Slap him upside the head! Kick him back to Venus!"

They start to form a circle around me.

Scott looks around at them and then back at me. He's grinning, but his black eyes have sharpened. "Yeah, sure, I'll get him."

I attempt to run away, but a little kid in the circle sticks out his leg and trips me.

I stumble and start to go down, and before I can get up Scott is on my back. He rides me to the ground, folds his hand into fists, and hammers me.

"You win," I say, desperately recalling all that I know about violent male pack behavior. "I lose. You are an alpha male, far stronger and better equipped than I am in the battle for survival of the fittest. You will mate and have progeny. I will be alone and cast out."

The circle of kids hoots at this. "You hear that? Survival of the fittest! Alpha male! What an alien!"

Scott draws back his fist. "Show us you're an alien. Eat dirt."

Dirt is, of course, not a substance that the human body can digest.

I quickly access the consciousness of Tom Filber. *How should I handle this?*

Do whatever he says. Otherwise he's going to bash your head in.

Scott's right fist is poised to strike. I stick out my tongue, hesitate, and then lick the ground.

Kids laugh. "How does it taste, Alien?" Scott demands.

I spit and gag.

"You don't like dirt? Try some grass. I better see you swallow it!"

I lower my head again, bite off a blade of a mono-cotyledonous green plant in the family Gramineae, and chew on it.

"Look, he's doing it!" one of the young onlookers calls out delightedly.

"Maybe he'll give milk next," somebody else suggests, and laughs ring out.

Scott gets up off me and rubs his hands together, as if scraping off dust after a job. Then he looks around at the circle of kids. "Anybody says anything about this at school, it's their turn next," he warns. He points a finger at one boy whose face is scarred with the lesions and cysts of acne vulgaris, a skin condition that often affects young humans. "You understand that, Zitface?"

The boy called Zitface's eyes are gleaming with excitement, and I can tell he enjoyed watching the beating. "I didn't see anything," Zitface says. "I wasn't even here."

8

I lie there, unmoving, till I am sure Scott is far away. Then I spit out the grass and take an inventory of my body. I am sore where he punched me, but no bones are broken.

Still, I have had enough. Much more than enough. No Sandovinian has been treated this way in all of recorded history. I have just been victimized by a "bully"—an overly aggressive young Earthling who attempts to conceal his own weakness and insecurities by picking on those he deems even more vulnerable. I remember the feel of the Earthling bully on top of me, pinning me down. I vividly recall the bloodthirsty faces of the crowd, urging him on to inflict greater pain. And I will not soon forget being forced to eat dirt.

I am a Level-Five GC Evaluator, trained to be sympathetic to new forms of behavior and to endure cultural surprises. But even I have my limits!

To hell with the human race. They do not deserve this green grass that they force each other to eat. They do not deserve the blue skies whose atmosphere they are sullying, or the lovely oceans they are befouling. And they certainly do not deserve this last fair chance that I and the GC were striving to give them.

I will text-message my spaceship and notify the Preceptors that the decision was an unexpectedly easy one: Destroy species Homo sapiens, and good riddance to them!

"Tom?" A kind, caring voice reaches out to me.

Give their lush planet to the Lugonians! One pulse of a carefully calibrated Gagnerian Death Ray will do the trick from Arctic to Antarctic!

"Tom, are you okay? Who are the Lugonians?"

A soft hand reaches down and brushes some gravel off my chin.

I look up into two bright blue eyes, bluer and deeper than the sky overhead. "No," I tell her, "I said it feels like I got hit with a sack of onions."

"Quit staring at me like that!"

"Like what?"

"Get this straight. I'm just doing this because I feel sorry for you and you happen to be my neighbor. Are you bleeding?"

I shake my head. So this is Michelle Peabody.

She has silky blond hair that moves in the breeze. Remarkably, even as I lie beaten and bruised and condemning the entire species, I feel a sharp spike of human testosterone. It is in fact a stronger chemical than I thought, but I easily vanquish it. "Thank you for your concern," I tell her. "I will be okay."

"No, you won't. Tom, sit up. Listen to me. You can't let Scott do that to you. Why don't you fight back?"

"He's stronger than I am."

"It doesn't matter. If you fight back, he'll stop bullying you."

"Or he might kill me."

"I just don't get what's wrong with you," she says. She glances quickly at her watch. "Uh-oh! Five minutes to get to school. Come on!"

9

"To be, or not to be," Mrs. Hilderlee enthuses, jabbing a finger at us. "*To be, or not to be!* It is the single most famous line ever written in the English language. What do you think Shakespeare was trying to say to us?"

I am sitting in fourth-period English with twenty of my classmates, including my tormentor, Scott, his peon, Zitface, and lovely Michelle Peabody, in a trailer that has been converted to a classroom. Winthrop P. Muller High School is apparently too small to accommodate all the offspring of the testosterone-fueled citizens of the town of Barrisford, so they have expanded into old trailers in the parking lot.

"Hey, Alien," Zitface whispers. "To be or not to be dead meat in gym class? I think to be."

I ignore him. I am busy trying to unravel the great mystery of "school." It is clearly more complicated than mere voluntary incarceration. Now that I have spent a night with the Filber family, I have some new insights into this puzzling institution. I believe the real premise behind "school" has to do with the fact that Planet Earth is very beautiful, and there are many pleasant things to do on it. But the reality is that most of the students in Barrisford will never get to do any of those things.

They will not visit beautiful places. They will not think deep thoughts and have exciting adventures. Their jobs will be tedious and they will come home at the end of each day consumed by fury like my mother or trying to put their brains to sleep like my dad.

Scott grins at me. "How did you like your breakfast?"

"Excuse me. I am listening to our teacher."

"Plenty more where that came from, Alien. I'm not finished with you yet."

Mrs. Hilderlee must be a bit deaf, because she does not hear the class bully's threats. She is standing by the trailer's lone window with a faraway look on her face. I believe she has taught this same lesson so many times that she is capable of doing it completely on autopilot. "I want everyone to write down five 'To be, or not to be' moments from your own lives," she says. "If Shakespeare could do it, you can, too."

The students around me groan and grimace.

"If Shakespeare was here, I'd kick him in the gonads," Scott mutters.

All around me kids chew gum, pass notes, and steal glances at the large clock on the wall. No one writes anything.

Scott whispers something to Michelle Peabody. I hear the words "movie" and "hang out." She blushes and shakes her head. "I told you no a hundred times."

"Don't be a tease," he whispers back. "You know you like me."

I try to ignore this, and concentrate on my mission. I have only been to three classes on this, my first day at school, but I have already seen enough to begin forming a new hypothesis. My new theory is that school serves the purpose of narrowing the horizons of young Homo sapiens and conditioning them to accept mediocrity as their birthright and drudgery as their lot. The teachers accomplish this by taking the most beautiful creations of the human mind, and the sharpest insights by human thinkers in a variety of fields, and boiling them down to a nonsensical pabulum that they feed to their students year after year till the children of Barrisford are convinced that there is nothing out there worth striving for.

By the time Scott, Zitface, and Michelle Peabody graduate, Winthrop P. Muller High School will have accomplished its mission and they will have stopped reading great books, caring about the brilliant insights of deep thinkers, and dreaming their own dreams. Their brains will have been dulled and their ambitions dampened, and they will be ready to shoulder the burden of a lifetime of hard work with few rewards.

Mrs. Hilderlee is, I believe, attempting to speed this process along right now by reducing Shakespeare's most famous play to sheer drivel. "To be, or not to be?" she repeats, gazing out the trailer's single gritty window. "To speak in class, or not to speak in class? Who is ready to share with us?"

She waits with an expectant smile planted on her face, but no one seems inclined to share this morning. "I need a volunteer," she says. "Otherwise I'll have to call on someone."

"Alien, raise your hand," Scott commands.

"But I don't have anything to say," I whisper back. "I am here to observe and learn."

"Raise your hand right now or I'll rip your arm out of its socket in gym class."

From my detailed knowledge of human anatomy, I can project that having my arm ripped from my socket would produce excruciating pain. I glance at Scott and he makes a violent ripping motion in the air. I hesitate a second more and reluctantly raise my hand.

"Thomas? Do you have a 'To be, or not to be' moment that we can all enjoy?"

"No," I tell her. "But I do have a question."

She looks startled. "Go on."

I glance at Scott and Zitface, and then back at her. "Do you think that the whole human race may hit a 'To be, or not to be' moment relatively soon?"

"I'm not sure I follow you," she says. "Why would we?"

I wish I could tell her that at this very moment a GC spaceship is orbiting Earth with a Gagnerian Death Ray on board. But of course that is not information I can reveal.

"Keep talking, Alien," Zitface hisses. "Just a few more minutes and we're free."

"My question is this," I tell her. "We are destroying our beautiful planet. We are building weapons of mass destruction. We are cruel to our fellow humans, and even nastier to our animal and fish neighbors. Doesn't it seem to you that, as a species, we may soon be facing a 'To be, or not to be' moment? We may destroy ourselves, or someone with greater power and wisdom may decide to put us out of our misery?"

Mrs. Hilderlee looks back at me, opens her mouth, and closes it again. "That is a very worrying suggestion," she finally says as the bell rings.

10

"Today in biology we are going to do a dissection," Mr. Karnovsky announces. "If you need to throw up, I have put a purple pail right over there, by the window. If you miss the pail, you will have to clean it up."

"Cool! Are we going to dissect human corpses?" Scott asks, picking up a small dissecting knife and waving it about like a sword.

"Put down that knife before I call the security guard," Mr. Karnovsky orders. "There will be no human corpses today."

"How about a cat or a dog?" Zitface asks.

"We will work our way from simple organisms to more complex ones," Mr. Karnovsky informs him. "In that way our dissection experiences will give us a chance to appreciate how evolution leads to modification and complexity. We've talked about the theories of Charles Darwin."

A girl with frizzy red hair raises her hand. "Do we have to do this?"

"Of course," Mr. Karnovsky says. "It's mandatory."

"What if it's against my religion?"

"Why don't you just throw up right now and get it over with, Sue Ellen?" Zitface suggests.

"I will for sure if I look at you," she says back.

Some people laugh. Zitface does not like that. He is, apparently, quite sensitive about his appearance. "Watch out, freaky-haired bitch."

"What are you gonna do? Infect me with your zits?"

He kicks her chair so hard her head snaps back. "How do you like that?"

"Touch me again and my brother will kick your ass," she hisses.

I listen to the insults and threats flying back and forth between my classmates and try to figure out why they hate each other. It is a question at the very heart of my secret mission.

The Council of Elders stipulated three criteria that I must use in deciding whether the human race is worth preserving. First, I must determine whether the violent and cruel behavior manifested by adult humans is innate or acquired. As I sit listening to Sue Ellen and Zitface trade threats and insults, I recall the bloodthirsty faces of the youngest members of the crowd that witnessed my beating this morning.

The kid who tripped me couldn't have been more than ten. My strong impression so far is that humans are as mean at five as they are at fifty.

Mr. Karnovsky shouts, "ENOUGH! SHUT UP!" and

points to a sheet tacked to the bulletin board. "I've posted your lab partner assignments," he says. "Now, behave for just a moment. I'm going to get today's dissection cadavers." He ducks into an adjacent supply room, and the kids cluster around the bulletin board.

"No way I'm working with the Alien!" Zitface announces. He looks around and focuses on a thin boy who has a set of colored pens. "Peterson, you're switching with me."

Peterson shakes his head. "No way. I'm not working with the Alien."

"Did I give you a choice?"

"Did I give anyone a choice?" Mr. Karnovsky asks, returning to the room with two bulging sacks. Presumably whatever we are going to dissect is in those sacks. I notice that my classmates are suddenly fixated on them, trying to guess what it might be from the bumps and lumps.

"They're rats."

"No way, turtles."

"Snakes."

"Guinea pigs."

"Frogs."

Mr. Karnovsky pulls on some rubber gloves and a plastic face mask. "Before we embark on our journey of experimental inquiry, let us pause for an observation from the brilliant mind of Charles Darwin," he says.

He opens a well-thumbed book and begins to read in a monotone. " 'Thus, from the war of nature, from famine and death, the most exalted object which we are capable of conceiving, namely, the production of the higher animals, directly follows . . . from so simple a beginning endless forms most beautiful and wonderful have been, and are being, evolved.' "

My classmates are eager to begin dissecting and couldn't care less about the insights of Charles Darwin. But I try to ignore their jokes and spitballs and listen to Mr. Karnovsky's reading selection.

The second criterion that the Council stipulated I should use in deciding the fate of the human race is their capacity—or lack thereof—to create beauty or make original contributions to galactic knowledge. It would be uncivilized for the GC to destroy a species capable of profound aesthetic expression or scientific insight.

So far, in my humble estimation, Homo sapiens do not qualify on either count. William Shakespeare's "To be, or not to be" did not make too much of an impression on me. Now I listen to Mr. Karnovsky reading about Darwin and evolution, and how glorious it is that human beings are the highest animals. Meanwhile, Zitface is running through his repertoire of bathroom noises and Scott is making flushing sounds at appropriate intervals.

If this is the best the human race can do, the galaxy will surely not lose anything by eliminating them.

For just a moment, my eyes drift and meet the blue eyes of Michelle Peabody. She quickly looks up at the ceiling, as if counting the tiles there.

"Okay," Mr. Karnovsky announces, "let's get to it! Gloves and face masks on, please. I am now slitting the specimen bag open."

A strong, musky odor seeps out of the sack.

"OOOOHH. YUUUCK!" everyone seems to scream at once.

I actually find the aroma rather pleasant.

"It's slice-and-dice time," Scott calls out. "But what are they?"

"Molluscan class Gastropoda," Mr. Karnovsky tells us.

I immediately feel dizzy and almost topple to the floor. No. Please. Not that.

"We will begin with the muscular foot, which is lubricated with mucus for locomotion."

"No way I'm touching mucus!" a girl cries out.

"We will slit the body upward till we reach the front two antennae, also known as the eyestalks, where we will tweezer off the eyes," Mr. Karnovsky explains.

I am holding my stomach with both hands.

He picks the bag up by the bottom and tips it over.

"WORMS!" kids call out, guessing incorrectly. "GRUBS! WEEVILS!"

"No, slugs," Mr. Karnovsky corrects them. "Snails without shells."

I cannot stop myself from pointing out in a weak voice, "But they're still alive."

"Not a problem," Mr. Karnovsky notes. "We will start by pinning them to the dissection boards like this."

I watch his long pin descend toward what could well be my distant cousin. I try to control my reaction. I am, after all, on a secret mission. But I don't even make it to the purple pail by the window.

"Hey, LOOK!" Scott shouts out gleefully. "THE ALIEN IS BLOWING FLAGRANT CHOW ALL OVER MICHELLE'S SHOES!"

I am crouching down, retching uncontrollably. Poor Michelle Peabody is pinned between two desks, with no way to escape. I look up for a second into her horrified blue eyes and try to stammer out an apology. "I'm sorry. I can't . . ." Then another wave of nausea sweeps over me and my stomach seems to open up and void itself.

Michelle screams in horror, "STOP IT, YOU ALIEN!"

11

What happened to you in biology today could happen to anyone," the young woman in the green sweater says. She flashes me a confiding smile. "I always hated dissecting things. Frogs. Mice. Even snails."

We are in a small, bright office that looks down on ball fields. Kids are playing soccer below us. I see white netting blowing in the autumn wind.

"Snails deserve respect, too," I tell her.

She nods thoughtfully. "You're right, snails are living creatures. You're a very sensitive boy, Tom. That's a good thing. But it can also be painful."

Miss Schroeder is the psychologist at Winthrop P. Muller High School, which means she is an evaluator of kids with problems. Little does she know she is sitting across from a Level-Five GC Evaluator charged with deciding the fate of the human race! "We heard an unconfirmed report that there was some trouble this morning on the way to school," she tells me, watching my face carefully. "Do you want to tell me what happened?"

I am tempted to describe being forced to eat grass. But I recall Scott's warning to the circle of kids. I must obey the conventions of male adolescents.

I access the consciousness of Tom Filber. *Should I tell her?* I ask him.

His response comes back loud and clear from the Ragwellian Bubble: *If you squeal, you're toast.*

I give Miss Schroeder a shrug. "I appreciate your concern. It was nothing of great consequence."

She studies me, a bit intrigued. "Small things can be hurtful, too. I understand you have a nickname. Nicknames can be fun. But they can also be cruel."

"They call me Alien."

"I'm sorry. That must hurt."

Due to the coincidence of my taking over the body of an outsider, I can answer truthfully without compromising the secrecy of my mission. "No, they're right. I am an alien."

"When we're in our teens, we all feel that way from time to time," Miss Schroeder says gently. "But why do *you* feel they're right, Tom? Is it a lack of friends?"

On Sandoval IV, I have hundreds of dear old chums in every mud cluster. My GC friends and colleagues number in the thousands and are scattered across the galaxy. But here on Planet Earth, I'm surrounded by bullies and louts who treat me in cruel and illogical ways that I cannot comprehend. "Sometimes I feel isolated here," I admit.

"So you think you don't have much in common with your peers?"

My dear woman, I am a Sandovinian! I resemble a large Earth snail, I am more than two thousand years old, and I have an intellectual ability roughly thirty times that of an Earthling. "Not too much."

"Tom, is your family close?"

I recall all my dear kinfolk back home. Is six hundred light-years close? "Not as close as I would like."

"What separates you?"

"Space."

She nods. "That's a good way of putting it. Simple, but I've never heard it before." She leans forward. "Have you ever thought of striking back against people at school who call you Alien?"

"No."

"Never considered bringing a weapon to school?"

The Gagnerian Death Ray is on the spaceship, orbiting Earth at an altitude of more than six miles. If it is used to destroy species Homo sapiens, I won't be the one calibrating it or flipping the switch. "Never."

"I was talking to your English teacher," Miss Schroeder continues. "You made a comment in class today about how we all might be destroyed soon."

I look back into her big brown eyes. Evaluation is challenging and a grave responsibility. She is obviously worried. I attempt to put her mind at ease. "My point in class was that we've done a lot of damage to our beautiful planet earth and we'd better be more careful."

"I couldn't agree more," Miss Schroeder says, and writes a few quick notes on the pad in front of her. "Tom, I'd like to make a suggestion. I see that you don't participate in any after-school activities. There's a new club forming. An environmental group called the Teen Green Team. Since you have this concern about our earth, you might find it interesting and make some friends. Will you think about joining?"

"I will consider it. Can I go now?"

She nods. "Let's talk again soon. My door is always open." She stands and I stand also. "And for what it's worth, I don't think you're an alien. I think you're a really nice, sensitive kid."

She holds out her right hand and I take it. You're quite mistaken, madam. I am a snail creature from a planet of oozing red mud in a distant nebula. "Thanks."

12

The bell rings, and a thunderous stampede immediately begins. We are free! I am caught up in the wild rush and feel an unexpectedly powerful sense of liberation. The oppressive, brain-shrinking voluntary incarceration is over for the day!

Out the exits we stream, down the steep stone steps of Winthrop P. Muller High School we scamper, and soon we are escaping down the hill. Most of the kids are walking in knots and bunches, with their friends.

I hurry home alone. I am grateful that Tom Filber is an alien. If I had inhabited the body of a boy with many friends, I would have to pretend to fit into his social network. I do not need a new challenge right now.

School has provided quite enough excitement for one day. I am looking forward to exploring Barrisford on my own. Also, I feel a strong need for a Flindarian Lapse, and that can only be accomplished in complete privacy.

As I walk home, I notice several kids riding swiftly by

on primitive pedal-driven two-wheeled vehicles known as "bikes," propelling themselves with aggressive movements of their legs. I access the consciousness of Tom Filber. *Have you such a vehicle?*

Piece of junk. In the garage, comes the unenthusiastic response from the Ragwellian Bubble.

When I reach the Filber residence I head into the garage. It is an old wooden structure in a state of disrepair. The door does not have a lock, which on Planet Earth suggests that nothing valuable is stored inside. Tom Filber must be right that his bicycle is a less than desirable model.

There are rusty tools and crude implements for cutting grass, raking leaves, and shoveling snow. I see deflated automobile tires and a pile of broken bricks. A tiny animal flees from me in terror. This is an example of order Rodentia, family Muridae—a mouse.

There is a pungent chemical smell in the garage. I push my way through the junk and spot cans of chemicals and dusty old glass beakers. They have been stored beneath a long workbench that is completely covered over with junk. Someone in the Filber family once tinkered here.

I inhale the stench of the chemicals and use a Ganchian Deductive Process to ascertain their composition. There are pigments, resins, and binders. Taken together, they are the ingredients of a liquid that can be applied to a substrate in a thin layer—commonly known as paint. I wonder who experimented with paints in this old garage.

Ah, here is Tom's bike, hanging from two pegs. It is

indeed not a new or impressive piece of machinery. The metal surfaces are dented, dinged, and rusted. But it appears functional.

I carry it outside the garage and get on. Balancing on a bicycle is not as easy as it looks. I almost fall off, and barely manage to catch myself by hurriedly putting down a leg.

"Hey, Four Eyes, did you forget how to ride a bike?"

It is my sister, walking home from school with a tall friend.

"No, I did not forget," I tell her, "but thank you for your concern."

"Your brother's weird," the tall girl observes. "I hear he tossed his cookies in science class today."

"He's such a loser," Sally says, and she seems to speak extra loud to ensure that I can hear her words. "My mom and dad wish they could just put him back and pick again."

The tall girl chuckles. "That's harsh."

I have figured out how to balance on the bicycle and glide by her. "Goodbye, sister," I say. "As you can see I am quite a good bicycle rider."

"What a freak show," Sally grunts to her friend.

I pedal into the street and pick up speed. This primitive locomotive device is unexpectedly pleasurable to ride. The breeze blows in my face, and the handles that I am gripping vibrate slightly with the irregularities in the pavement of Beech Avenue.

I take one hand off experimentally and wave it around. The balancing is much harder, but I manage it. Ta-da! I head downhill and glide. Yes, this is quite pleasant indeed. The trees appear to reach across Beech Avenue and shake hands overhead.

It is time for me to find a private spot and enjoy a nice Flindarian Lapse.

13

pedal the old bike to River Road and follow the bank of the Hoosaguchee northward. Factories spew out smog into the blue afternoon sky. I can smell the river, and it is not a particularly pleasant aroma.

How beautiful this must once have been, and how species Homo sapiens has fouled it up! In the entire galaxy, no other semi-intelligent species has ever been so foolish as to almost destroy the very place where it lives!

This is the third and final criterion the GC Preceptors have told me to use in deciding the fate of the human race. I must deduce whether it is inevitable that humans will ruin Planet Earth, or if it is still possible that they will recognize their folly and pull back from the brink. If the former, we owe it to the multitude of other life-forms here to transfer management to a wiser steward race.

I pass Kinderly Plastics Works. R&Z Refrigeration. A gray behemoth topped by twin smokestacks looms with a sign that reads HARBISHAW INDUSTRIAL PAINTS.

A wire fence with sharp spikes encloses the facility. My father mentioned the name Harbishaw, and there were the chemical ingredients for mixing paints in our garage. I wonder what my dad's connection is to this forbidding factory.

I reach the end of River Road and leave my bike beneath a tree. No one ever stole it from the Filbers' unlocked garage, so it seems unlikely that anyone would pilfer it in this remote spot.

I walk along the muddy, pebble-strewn bank. Amazingly, there is still much wildlife here. Frogs croak at me. A black-clawed mud crab pops out of the muck to squint at me and then quickly sinks back out of sight. In the river, a tiny brown fish with what looks like a silver sequin sewn onto its belly surfaces for a second and reflects sunlight in my direction.

Gray river mud squishes beneath my feet. I almost feel like I am home.

I choose a spot beneath two weeping willow trees whose long branches dangle to the grass and blot out the factories.

Birds warble from high above. Flies and gnats buzz all around me.

I lie back on the grass and close my eyes. For a long moment, the Lapse eludes me. Instead, the day's worst moments vividly recur and swirl around.

I recall how it felt when Scott was on top of me, hammering me while young kids egged him on. I remember throwing up on Michelle's shoes.

As these painful recollections come back, the Hoosa-guchee River seems to rise up from the bank. I have the strange sensation that it seeps toward me in a noxious cloud of foul odors and toxins. The smell is acrid, biting. I tear up and gasp for a breath of fresh air. I seem to hear the different life-forms in the river—the fish, the frogs, and even the bugs—crying out to me in pain and misery.

A cool breeze blows and the awful smell dissipates. I try to concentrate on the sweet aroma of river mud, and on the trees and flowers.

I force the bad memories away and wipe my mind blank. All I hear now are the chirping of the birds and the thrumming of the insects. The breeze blows through me. I reach down deep into myself for the very essence of Ketchvar, and free myself from all boundaries.

Gone are the physical limitations of a boy with metal braces and ocular aids, and also of a snail creature that needs a shell at all times.

I float up through space. Ah, here is the ship, six miles above Earth, floating high above a mantle of white clouds. I melt inside and see my fellow crewmen going about their jobs. The Preceptor Supervisor is briefing GC Command. "First day of school is complete," he is saying. "We're waiting for the report."

The Preceptor is a five-legged Turkloid from Omicron II, with a scaly, orange-yellow face. He clearly doesn't like what he's hearing back from the GC Supervisors.

"Of course I realize that the Lugonians are impatient," he responds. "I would be too, if my sun were about to supernova. But I remind you that this mission was authorized by a full vote of the Senior Council. Ketchvar is very able, and we must give him the time he needs."

I cannot interact in any way during a Flindarian Lapse, or I would thank him for the vote of confidence.

I pass on through the ship and see the Mission Engineers at their control panels, and the long shaft of the Gagnerian Death Ray with its shiny hood. Its monitor has been calibrated, and I see that the controls have already been set for all human DNA vectors. One touch of the glowing red button, a single violet pulse-flash, and it will all be over for the human race.

I melt out of the spaceship and hurl myself homeward. Stars swirl by me like snowflakes. They merge into a milky streak of white traced against a long wall of black.

And then two scarlet pinpricks in the distance. The twin suns of Sandoval IV!

I float down. It is evening, and the mud glows a cheerful shade of red.

As the sunlight recedes, the time of the Great Evening Squeak approaches.

Sandovinians crawl to the surface, stopping to greet each other. Those traveling longer distances zip through the air on silver floaters.

Here is Mud Cluster Seven in the Chigaboid Quadrant. I sink down into the cool clay to the Ketchvar burrow. The familiar tunnels of home open before me!

I glimpse dear faces. Ketchvar II is crawling a little slower these days but the crystalline eyes at the top of each cephalic tentacle are as bright as ever. He reaches the surface just in time.

The Squeak has begun! Millions of Sandovinians are lying in the shallow, cool water, sliding back and forth in their shells, forcing the air out in controlled puffs, celebrating and communing. Each whistle and squeak is a personal song, a sculpture of movement, a thread in the tapestry.

I float above the red ooze, and my essence becomes one with the Squeak. The great ideas of Sandoval are part of that squeak, and the news of the day, and the joyful birth announcements. There is a marvelous sharing . . .

The Squeak suddenly goes silent, and a voice like a sweeping wind whooshes out, "Answer me!"

The twin red suns dwindle to distant embers and blink out. I am yanked away willy-nilly through the cosmos against my will. This has never happened to me before! Such a precipitous withdrawal from a Flindarian Lapse is extremely dangerous, and can even be fatal.

The stars cascade into froth, the blackness of space swallows me in a sucking gulp, and I fear I will crash out and dissolve.

A voice demands, "What the hell are you doing here? Wake up and answer me or I'll turn you over to the cops!" A hand shakes me hard.

I blink, disoriented, and look up into the angry face of a large man in a gray uniform.

14

I must have fallen asleep," I tell the man. "Who are you?"

He looks enraged at the question. "I'm a security guard, get it?"

I am still recovering from my forced withdrawal from the Flindarian Lapse. "Do I get what?"

"Are you trying to be a wise guy?"

"No, sir."

When I call him sir, he releases his grip on my shirt. "Don't you know this is private property?"

"No, sir."

"Well there are signs posted. Harbishaw Paints owns all the land to the river. What the hell are you doing here?"

I shrug, wondering why a paint factory requires such privacy. "Nothing. Just experiencing a lapse."

He squints down at me. "Well, go home and snooze in your bed. Dogs patrol the factory grounds at night. They're mean critters. Believe me, you wouldn't want to have one of them biting you in the butt."

"I believe you." I stand up. "I will endeavor to follow all regulations in the future."

"Make sure you do that," he says. "Git out of here!"

I return to my bike and pedal toward home. I look back once over my shoulder and see the twin smokestacks of the Harbishaw paint factory belching black smoke into the clear sky.

The afternoon is giving way to evening. There is of course no Great Squeak here on Planet Earth, but the sky is turning a dark purple color and it is very pleasant. I see no kids out on the street. They must be home, eating dinner with their families.

I stow my bike in the garage and prepare to enter the Filber residence, but I stop when loud voices ring out from inside. "IF YOU DON'T LIKE TURKEY MEAT LOAF, NOBODY'S FORCING YOU TO EAT IT!" my mother screams.

"I like turkey meat loaf fine," my father says back. "I only meant it seems like we're having it every night—"

"WELL, WHY DON'T YOU COOK SOMETHING? OR EVEN BETTER, WHY DON'T YOU BRING HOME SOME DECENT MONEY AND THE MEAL PLAN AROUND HERE MIGHT IMPROVE."

"I'm looking for work."

"Yeah, well, don't look too hard. You might actually find some."

"Ruth, cut me a break—"

"YOU GIVE ME A BREAK."

"NO, YOU GIVE ME A BREAK!"

My sister's voice joins the hubbub. "WILL YOU TWO SHUT UP? I'M TRYING TO DO HOMEWORK."

"THAT'S NO WAY FOR A DAUGHTER TO SPEAK TO HER FATHER."

"SHE'S RIGHT. YOU SHOULD SHUT UP."

"MOM, HE HAS A POINT, TOO. THAT TURKEY MEAT LOAF IS WORSE THAN DOG FOOD."

Much as I am sure I would enjoy sampling the turkey meat loaf with my delightful family, I decide not to enter the house right now. Instead I stroll into the backyard. The crab apple tree is stirring in the wind, and a tiny apple drops off and hits me in the head. As I bend to pick it up, I glimpse movement through a gap in the hedge.

A primitive wooden contraption with two benches is moving back and forth in the Peabody backyard. I believe it is known as a swing, due to its lateral movement.

I walk closer to investigate. It is a simple device, hung from a tree branch. Inside the carriage part of the swing are two wooden benches facing each other. Michelle Peabody is sitting on one of those benches, pushing a lever with her legs to make the swing move slowly back and forth.

I walk through the gap in the hedge and call out to her. "Greetings, Michelle. Do not be alarmed. It is not a stranger, come to harm you. It is only me, Tom Filber."

She is wearing jeans and a Windbreaker and eating an

apple. She cranes her head to peer at me. In the fading light of sunset, her blond hair looks like spun gold.

I walk up to the swing and stand before it, watching her glide back and forth. "How are you, Michelle?"

"What do you mean, how am I?"

"I mean, how are you feeling on this lovely evening?"

She lowers the apple and studies me for several seconds. "Fine. What about you? Are you still sick?"

"I am all better." I lower my hands to my sides and slightly incline my head in a posture humans find penitent. "I'm sorry I threw up on your shoes today."

"You should be." Then she shrugs. "Don't worry about it. Those snails were pretty gross."

"Snails deserve respect, too," I tell her. "Can I climb on the swing?"

She hesitates for several seconds. "If you want. Don't sit next to me. Sit on the other bench."

I sit down on the other bench and look across at her. "Is your apple delicious?"

"It's okay."

"How come you're sitting out here with a piece of fruit instead of having dinner with your family?"

"None of your business," Michelle says.

She looks away for a moment. Her face is tight with concealed pain. The swing, moving back and forth on the branch, makes an occasional high-pitched squeaking noise.

"My own family is having turkey meat loaf," I tell her. "My sister says it's worse than dog food. I would rather be sitting out here with you. Can I help push the swing?"

She looks back at me. "Uh-huh."

I put my feet on the other side of the lever. She pushes it toward me. I push it back to her. Our toes brush.

"There's a new club forming at school," I tell her. "It's an environmental group called the Teen Green Team. I am thinking of joining."

"I heard about it," she says.

"So are you thinking about joining, too?"

"No, I've got orchestra practice after school. Anyway, it sounds like kind of a waste of time to me. Things are so messed up. How can anyone make a difference?"

I look back at her and think about the last readings we took from space. Global warming melting the ice caps. Deforestation on every continent. Coral dying. Fish stocks crashing. Poor Planet Earth spiraling into ruin. "Maybe you're right."

"No, you should join," she says. "Seriously, you should try it." She hesitates a long beat. "Tom, I'm sorry I called you an alien."

"You were angry at me because of your shoes," I say. "I understand. I hope you were able to clean them."

"I just threw them out."

"Human vomit has an adhesive quality that makes it difficult to dissolve, but warm water and soap would have done it."

Michelle takes another bite of the apple. Her blue eyes study my face. "Can I ask you a question?"

"Please."

"Don't take this the wrong way. Why are you so weird?"

"I don't understand."

"Do you intentionally try to act weird? Or is that just the way you really are?"

I wish I could answer Michelle's question truthfully. I would like to tell her about the Galactic Confederation and its wise and benevolent policies. If she knew that there were thousands and thousands of gentle and peaceful life-forms out there, watching over and helping each other, she might be able to go into her house and have dinner with her family and sleep better at night.

I would also enjoy telling her about some of the beautiful things I've seen on my space voyages. This sunset on Planet Earth is quite pleasant, but it doesn't compare to the rainbow twilight of Tau Ori or the pink comet showers of Kaus Meridianalis.

But of course I can't tell her any of these things. All I can do is hint at the truth. "It's just the way I am."

"Why?" she asks. "I've lived next to you all my life and I just don't get it."

"I guess I'm not like everybody else," I tell her in a whisper. "I look at life on Planet Earth a little differently."

She finishes the apple and flips the core into the gathering darkness. "But why? You haven't answered my question."

I look back at her, open my mouth, and then close it again. The metal swing brackets scrape over the tree branch above our heads.

"Okay," she finally says. "None of my business, right? It's getting cold. We'd better go in."

15

To: reveredelders@galacticconfederation.com
Subject: How to Sauté a Skunk

Revered Galactic Confederation Elders. I am once again en-
crypting this entry, using a file name that no Earthling will be
tempted to scan.

My first day on Planet Earth is finally over. This is indeed a
cruel and violent place.

All is now silent in the Filber home, but two hours ago there
was a terrible fight between my mother and father. It took
place in their bedroom so I did not witness the encounter, but
I could tell by the cries and sounds of breaking objects that it
quickly escalated into violence.

My sister finally started screaming for them to stop, and my
father fled out of the bedroom, up the stairs, into his attic

office. I believe he is still there, trying to put his brain to sleep with late-night TV.

GC ethicists may be right that we should eliminate the human race before new weapons of mass destruction wreak havoc on the weak, or destroy the global environment, but after my first day on Planet Earth, I see another reason we may need to use the Gagnerian Death Ray. All humans seem to live in such a perpetual state of pain that putting them out of their misery would be an extremely merciful act.

I am not speaking merely of physical pain. Every person I have gotten to know so far seems to be lonely, confused, and wallowing in sadness and regret. There is no logical reason for such pervasive torment. Humans seem inclined to create for themselves as much suffering as they can possibly endure, and sometimes even a trifle more.

As I write this on Tom Filber's laptop computer, my right leg is stretched out on a chair, with an ice bag above the kneecap. Tom's body sustained several cuts and bruises when I was beaten on the way to school this morning. I have applied primitive human medical techniques such as ice, disinfectant, and Band-Aids to these wounds, but they still hurt.

I am willing to suffer pain and indignity to complete my GC mission, but I now see that there is a serious risk of being maimed or even killed by an enraged Earthling. I have therefore decided to carry my Emergency Contact Wibbler with me at all times. I am encasing my ECW inside an old package of miniature sugar doughnuts so it will escape detection by an overly inquisitive Earthling. If I am threatened with imminent annihilation, I will wibble the spaceship at our prearranged decimeter band frequency.

Please respond immediately. If I send an emergency wibble, it means the situation is dire.

Speaking of dire situations, I have just finished reading the new Lugonian plea for the immediate extinction of Homo sapiens and the resettlement of Planet Earth. It must be terrifying when one's home star stops generating energy from nuclear fusion. I feel for the young Lugonians, living under the constant threat that their sun will experience gravitational collapse into a black hole.

I have known several Lugonians and found them to be among the most charming and gentle creatures in the galaxy. There is no doubt in my mind that if they inherited this jewel of a planet they would quickly clean it up and cherish it. The endangered life-forms on Planet Earth would thrive under their wise stewardship.

Nevertheless, humans got here first. They are native to this world, and they cannot be exterminated merely out of sympathy for the Lugonians. I will require a little more time to complete my evaluation.

For a species of such limited intelligence, humans are surprisingly complicated. I have experienced their cruelty firsthand and my body literally bears the scars, but I have also seen that some members of the species are capable of friendly and generous behavior. My neighbor is a kind girl, and Miss Schroeder, the school psychologist, was attempting to help me. I must not be rushed to judgment in condemning them all.

It is now two in the morning and I am online and wearing earphones. I have listened to every song in Tom Filber's extensive music collection. These fall into three genres: hip-hop, punk, and industrial. As I write this, I am listening to a gangster rapper named Shorty D. Long singing about putting a cap in his ho.

One can draw a straight line from the epics of Homer to this rap song by Shorty D. Long. All of human art seems dedicated to the glorification of violence and the romanticization of the impulse to procreate. The first is frequently called warfare and the second is known as love. They are both, of course, empty and artificial constructs.

Today in class I was introduced to William Shakespeare's plays. I am now perusing them online. They are full of brutal violence and frustrated lovers.

I have just finished reading *Romeo and Juliet*, the most famous human love story. These two teenagers are so infatuated with each other they both end up dead for no reason at all! Romeo poisons himself and kisses Juliet. Juliet wakes up, sees that he is dead, and kisses him to try to share the poison. Only human beings would try to invest two teenagers' hormonal attraction to each other, culminating in a simple touching of the lips, with such absurd dramatic poignancy.

The body of Tom Filber requires at least a few hours' sleep a night, so I will sign off in just a moment.

I look out the window and see that the light has finally been turned off in Michelle Peabody's bedroom across the way. I wonder what kept her awake so long into the night? Perhaps it was the same thing that kept her out on the swing during dinnertime.

I wonder what her bedroom looks like. Pink seems to be a color that many girls favor. But Michelle doesn't seem to me like a pink girl.

But I digress, venerable Elders. Please assure the Preceptors that I am focused and hard at work. Today was a big first step. Tomorrow I will no doubt gain a much keener appreciation of what it means to be human.

Please keep monitoring for my emergency wibble. Suburban New Jersey turns out to be a war zone, and I may require your intervention at any moment.

Signing off now. Your humble evaluator, Ketchvar III.

16

Earth mission, day two. I am a little more careful about walking to school. Avoid bullies. Don't take shortcuts through secluded alleyways. When necessary, duck behind trees and let obnoxious classmates pass by. This is known as street smarts. I, Ketchvar III, am learning to survive on Planet Earth.

I see some older teenagers coming and hear their raised voices. Ah, here's a convenient member of family Fagaceae, genus Quercus. I duck behind the large oak tree and wait for them to pass.

A few seconds later I hear a deep voice. "Hey, slow down, Flabber, I mean Filber. I just want to talk to you. You owe me twenty dollars."

I hear my sister's voice answer, "I don't owe you anything. I wrote the paper."

"Yeah, but I didn't pay twenty dollars for a C."

"We can get low grades on our own, Boulder Butt," another voice chips in. There is mocking laughter.

I peek out from behind the tree and see that three boys, even bigger than Scott, are walking right behind my sister. She holds her cello in one hand, keeps her head down, and tries to walk very fast.

The tallest of the boys has a baby face, sandy brown hair, and enormous biceps. He grabs her backpack and tugs on it. "Where's my twenty bucks? Did your old man find it and piss it away already? I saw him yesterday at the Emerald Tavern. He was having a liquid lunch. Is that his office?"

My sister tries to walk away from them, but the big kid is not letting go of her backpack. "Whoa, Nellie. Did anyone give you permission to leave? I want my money back, and I'm not playing around."

I recall how it felt when Scott was picking on me and no one came to my aid. There is no one on this street who can help my sister except me.

I spot a single-seeded nut of genus Quercus on the ground, encased in a cup-shaped cupule. I bend and pick up the acorn and hold it in my hand. As an evaluator it is my duty to observe but not interfere. On the other hand, she is my sister.

"I wrote you an A paper," Sally says. "It's not my fault if Mr. Sanderson's an idiot." She tries to sound calm, but I hear panic in her voice.

"Whose fault is it?" the big kid demands. "You didn't do the job. Give me back my money or this is gonna get ugly fast."

Sally tries to get away but he won't let go. His friends laugh as she gets more and more upset.

"Watch out, Jace. She might sit on you."

I access the consciousness of Tom Filber. *Should I throw the acorn and try to distract them?*

Are you crazy? comes the response. *That's Jason Harbishaw. He's the worst bully in the whole high school. Stay hidden! Just be glad it's not you.*

But she's my sister. There's a family bond.

There's no bond. She hates your guts. Let her take her lumps.

Sally yanks hard on her backpack to try to free it, and it pops open. Books and papers fly out and land all over the ground. "Now look what you've done, Flabber," Jason says. "Here, let me help you pick that up." He pretends to help but kicks a book out of Sally's hand.

"STOP IT!" Her voice starts to crack apart.

I step out from behind the tree and hurl the acorn. This is the first time that I, Ketchvar III, have ever tried to intentionally harm a fellow living creature. I hate to admit this, but as the acorn connects with Jason's head I feel a thrilling sense of satisfaction. I can only conclude that having assumed the body of a human being, I am now subject to their primitive bellicose impulses.

"Ouch," Jason shouts. "What the hell was that?"

I duck back behind the tree.

"What was what, bud?" his friend asks.

"Something whacked me in the head!"

"It was just a stupid acorn, dude. There it is on the grass. It must have fallen off this tree."

"No, somebody winged it at me. It wasn't you two fools?"

"Not me," says fool number one.

"I didn't throw an acorn at you," the other chimes in.

"And it wasn't Boulder Butt," Jason notes. "Who else is here?"

They look around. I flatten myself up against the oak tree. Perhaps I should have followed Tom's advice. It appears that to survive and flourish as a human being on Planet Earth, it is a wise policy not to try to help someone else in trouble.

Footsteps approach. I have no place to hide. I consider pulling out my Emergency Contact Wibbler, but that would expose and terminate my mission and doom species Homo sapiens over a single thrown acorn. Surely I can find a way out of this on my own.

Jason spots me, grabs my arm, and drags me out of hiding. "Look what I found!"

"Unhand me," I say.

"I might un-head you," Jason growls. "Did you throw this acorn at me?"

I look back at him. "Yes."

"Why?"

"You were harassing my sister."

"Her ass *is* definitely pretty huge." Jason laughs.

Sally has now gathered up all her papers. She tries to sneak away while they're focused on me. "Hey, where are you running off to?" fool number one demands.

She glances at me. "He's the one who hit you with the acorn. Take it out on him!"

"I'm *gonna* take it out on him," Jason promises, and steps toward me with a cruel smile. "C'mere, punk."

EEE-EEEPPPP. EEE-EEEEPPP. A siren shrills from the street behind us. Jason instantly lowers his arm and drops the acorn. A police car has turned up the block. It pulls to a stop next to us. The window rolls down and a cop calls out, "Is there a problem here?"

"No, sir," Jason says. "We're on our way to school."

"Then get going," the cop says. "School is *that* way!"

Jason and his friends walk away.

The cop looks us over and frowns. "You're Graham Filber's kids, aren't you?"

Sally doesn't seem inclined to identify herself with me in any way. She busily checks her backpack to make sure all her papers are there.

"Yes, sir," I say. "He is our father and we are his offspring."

"I hear he's been hitting the sauce a little hard."

I am at a loss. "What is hitting the sauce?"

"Don't get smart with me. Tell your father to ease off the booze or Sergeant Collins is going to have to have a talk with him. Now off to school. Move it."

Sally and I hurry down the street. The police car trails us for a short while and then veers off.

I am alone with my sister.

"Are you okay?" I ask her.

She is walking with her head down, much the way she looked when she was trying to escape from the bullies.

"You should not be writing their papers in exchange for money," I advise her. "That is called plagiarism and it is a serious academic infraction."

She continues walking quickly, ignoring me.

"Don't let their insults bother you," I add. "There is no shame in having a prominent gluteus maximus. In many human cultures, a large buttock region is considered a desirable sign of strength and fertility in females."

She looks at me. "Do me a favor? Shut your mouth and spare me the sarcasm. And whatever you heard today about my business stays my business." Her eyes narrow dangerously. "If you breathe a word of it, I swear you'll regret it."

We walk on a bit. The brick facade of Winthrop P. Muller High School appears in the distance.

"Is our dad really hitting the sauce?" I ask her.

"Who knows and who cares. He's even more of a loser than you are."

The main entrance of our school is now visible. "Let me go in first," she says. "You stay back here. Don't let people see us together."

I stop walking. "Okay. Goodbye, Sally."

She takes two steps toward the school and then stops walking. She hesitates and then looks back at me. For one moment the mask of bitterness that she seems to wear at all times for self-protection falls away. "Why did you throw that acorn at Jason?"

"Because you are my sister and you needed help."

She considers this for a moment, and I see that my words

and my friendly tone almost get through to her. Then she pulls back, and the mask slams back across her face. "Yeah, right. Since when do you try to help me?"

I glance at my watch. "Since six minutes and twenty-seven seconds ago."

I see a glimmer of doubt on her face. Then it is replaced by her usual look of cold disdain. "Whatever game you're playing, give it up," she says. "'Cause it won't work. Don't follow me to school. Don't even talk to me. Keep your mouth shut about anything you heard. Just stay away from me."

17

The first meeting of the Teen Green Team takes place in a windowless basement room. I attempt to hide my excitement. This may turn out to be a highly valuable moment in my mission. The Lugonians argue persuasively that species Homo sapiens needs to be destroyed because they are ruining their planet and endangering millions of defenseless terrestrial and aquatic life-forms. But this club may provide evidence that the human race has recognized their folly and is now attempting to rectify the situation.

Six students trickle into the room. I only recognize one of them—Sue Ellen, from my biology class, with the frizzy hair. "Hi, Sue Ellen. I didn't know you were interested in the environment," I say.

"Don't talk to me. I'm having a bad day and I don't need a psycho pest buzzing around," she responds.

I consider pointing out that it will be difficult to band together and save the earth with an attitude like that, but I keep the observation to myself.

The boy sitting nearest to me is so skinny his ribs appear to poke through his green shirt. He glances at the clock every few seconds. "Well, I guess this isn't going to happen," he finally says, and stands up.

At that moment I hear a click-clicking noise just outside. The door opens and an old man walks in leaning heavily on a metal rod with wheels. A tank of what I believe is oxygen is fastened to the bottom of the walking-support mechanism. The white-haired man moves slowly and sucks air with difficulty. He pulls the door closed and glances around at us. "Only six? Well, I guess that's a start. Rome wasn't built in a day."

He walks very slowly to the front of the room, sits down in a chair, and inhales some more oxygen from the tank. We all watch him gasp and wheeze.

"He's gonna kick off right here," the tall thin kid whispers to a fat boy sitting next to him.

"That would get us out of school for sure!" the fat boy responds enthusiastically. "Witnessing death. Highly traumatic. Worth at least three days of home recovery time."

"You think so? Three days?"

"Definitely!"

The white-haired man takes out a handkerchief and dabs sweat off his brow; his hand trembles. Then he taps his fist on the desk. "My name is Arthur Stringfellow. I don't recognize any of you, but that's not surprising. They only let me teach one class these days."

Stringfellow has bushy white eyebrows that seem to rise

and lower for emphasis as he talks. "Let me tell you why I'm here. I guess you could see by watching me jog in that I've lost a few steps." He smiles at us. "This will be my last year teaching at Muller. My condition is degenerative. I'm slowly winding down, like an old clock. That's okay. I've had a good long run and I've enjoyed every tick and tock of it."

"He *is* gonna kick off!" the tall boy whispers.

"Not right now," the fat one responds. "Degenerative means it could take a while."

"Not the way he looks, bud."

Stringfellow doesn't seem to hear this exchange of whispers. He looks out at us and manages a sad smile. "When you're about to lose something, you appreciate it more," he tells us. "Teachers don't make a lot of money, but they get long vacations, and my wife and I have put those to good use. We've hopped around this globe a bit."

The door opens. A new student stands half in shadow.

"The show's already started," Stringfellow wheezes. "In or out, please."

Michelle Peabody steps hesitantly into the room. "I can't stay for long," she explains.

"Then stay for short," Stringfellow suggests.

I try to catch Michelle's eye. Did she come here because I said I was coming? She stays standing near the door and doesn't look at me.

Stringfellow's trembling hands move as he conjures something imaginary between his palms. It's a sphere—the round globe of Planet Earth. "It's a remarkably beautiful world," he notes, looking around at us. "But it's not mine anymore. I've got one step out the door. It's yours. And you're going to have to fight for it!"

I am disappointed to see that even a public-spirited and selfless man like Arthur Stringfellow links his hopes of saving the earth to violent notions of warfare. Nevertheless, his motives are admirable, and he appears to be a visionary. I wonder if all humans become less cruel and shortsighted as they near the moment of their demise.

Stringfellow peers around, as if to see what soldiers have enlisted in his little army. "I decided to start this club so we could do our bit," he explains. "That's why I'm here. What about the rest of you?" He looks at a boy in the very back of the room, with a skateboard on his lap.

"I got a D in earth science. My teacher said I'd get extra credit for coming."

"So you don't want to be here?" Stringfellow asks.

"You kidding? It's a perfect skateboarding day."

"Then get out."

"But my teacher said . . ."

"OUT!" Stringfellow half rises and his explosion of anger is truly frightening.

The skateboarder darts through the door and vanishes.

One gone, six left.

Stringfellow sits back down and breaks into a long fit of coughing. His anger has drained him. For a moment he seems to sink into himself.

"He's history," the thin boy whispers to his corpulent neighbor. "Get the pine box."

"No, he'll pull out of it."

"Bet you a dollar he croaks right here."

"You mean, right here right now?"

"Right here right now. You in or out?"

"In."

"Show me the buck."

"I don't have it right now."

"Deal's off."

Stringfellow finally manages to stop coughing and looks around at the rest of us. "Why are you here?" he asks Sue Ellen.

"I like cats," she says. "I've got four of them."

"Four cats gets you in the door," he says.

The girl next to Sue Ellen is dressed all in black and has her face buried in her arms on the desk. She feels the old man's gaze and looks up at him. "I'm Merrilee."

"What brings you to the Teen Green Team?"

"I'm a vegan. I used to eat chicken and fish, but I gave those up. Now I mostly just eat raisins and nuts. Kids tease me. They call me Fruit Bat."

"Fruit Bat, you can hang in our cave," Stringfellow tells her, and moves on to Michelle Peabody, who is still standing near the door. "Latecomer, what's your story?"

"Normally I have orchestra," Michelle tells him. "But Mr. Simmons was sick today. I heard about this new club and I just wanted to check it out."

"Why don't you check it out from a sitting position?" he suggests.

Michelle Peabody hesitates and sits down at the desk

next to mine. She is wearing white sneakers without socks, and I see that she has tiny freckles on her ankles.

Stringfellow moves on to the fat boy. "Young man?"

"Ralph Gurz. They cut down my tree."

"Your tree?"

"This tree I always used to climb. In Beaverdale Park. They just sawed it down."

"Who sawed it down?"

"I don't know who. One day I climbed it. The next day it was a stump."

"Welcome to the club." Stringfellow nods and looks at the tall thin kid.

"Green is my favorite color," the thin kid grunts.

"That's it?"

"It's been my favorite color since I was five."

"It's my favorite color, too," Stringfellow tells him.

Then he turns to me. "I hope we've saved the best for last. What's your story?"

I return his look. "I would like to see if humans appreciate Planet Earth enough to fight for it."

Stringfellow thinks my answer over. He peers back at me from under his bushy eyebrows. "That's an interesting sentiment, but it's very oddly expressed. You sound like you're excluding yourself from the battle."

"He's an alien!" Ralph Gurz whispers.

The old man shrugs. "There is no acceptable excuse for opting out of this struggle. I have the best excuse anyone could possibly have not to give a damn, and I still care. And if I do, you should, too. Yes?"

I look back at him. He's staring at me intently as he sucks oxygen. He is clearly dying. The fact that he cares so much for his planet, even in his last days, makes a great impression on me. I have seen the worst of humanity—their cruel, senseless, and violent behavior. Do I not also have an obligation as the evaluator charged with deciding the future of the human race to explore their best and most selfless impulses? Put simply, how will I be able to decide if the species has redeeming traits if I don't investigate and share its noblest struggle? "Yes," I say.

"In or out?"

"In, sir."

"Good." He nods. "Now, we can't reverse global warming here, or save the Amazon. But there's a lot of good work we can do much closer to home. So we're going to break up into pairs and pick different areas of town to work on. Cat girl, there are a lot of strays in the Swamouth Swamp. Do you and Fruit Bat want to tackle it?"

The two of them look at each other and nod.

"Ralph, since they cut down your tree, do you and Green Boy want to see what they left standing in Beaverdale Park?"

"Okay," Ralph says without too much enthusiasm.

The thin boy mutters, "Whatever."

"What about Mr. 'I'm Not Involved'?" Stringfellow asks, turning to me. "Any notion of what might inspire you to give a damn?"

I think of Jason the bully getting ready to beat me up over an acorn, and of the Harbishaw paint factory spewing smoke. "I'll take the Hoosaguchee River," I tell him, and throw a quick glance at Michelle.

"Excellent," Stringfellow says, noting the direction of my glance. "Orchestra Member, do you think you might find a little time to help him out?"

"I don't think so," Michelle answers. "We have a concert coming up and we're practicing all the time." She glances at me very quickly and then back at Stringfellow. "Anyway, that river's practically a sewer." She hesitates a few seconds more. "Well, I can't promise, but maybe I can help a little bit."

18

The Emerald Tavern is on Main Street. Above the entrance hangs a large green four-leaf clover, which some humans believe brings good luck. When I push in through the heavy door on my way home from school, I do not see many lucky-looking people inside.

The ceiling is low, the lighting is dim, and there is a musty smell. Sawdust covers the floor like a sprinkling of wooden snow. Eight men and two women sit on a row of stools facing a small TV, watching a baseball game and exchanging occasional conversation. Every now and then they raise glasses to lips in almost robotic movements.

The human tendency toward addictive and self-destructive behavior has been extensively observed, and now that I am inhabiting Tom Filber's body I have felt its pull myself. Tom ate several bags of potato chips every day, and since taking over his body I have experienced powerful cravings for dehydrated potato flakes. I have resisted because chips—whether salted or barbecued—have little nutritional value. Nevertheless, I have woken up in middle of the night thinking about ripping open a giant bag and stuffing handfuls in my mouth.

The ten adults drinking inside the Emerald Tavern are sipping a variety of alcoholic concoctions. They turn one by one to check me out. My father is not one of them.

A large man behind the bar who is cleaning glasses speaks to me. "We don't serve drinks to kids."

"I'm not thirsty," I tell him.

"That's Tom Filber's boy," somebody calls out.

"Is that right?" the big bartender asks. "Lookin' for your dad?"

"Yes, sir."

"He's paying his respects to the marble altar."

I do not understand this comment. "Excuse me?" I say. "Is my father involved in a religious ritual here?"

There are laughs from the customers.

"You could say that," the bartender says with a shrug. "He's kinda the high priest."

One guy on a stool says, "I heard Filber's boy has a screw loose."

"Don't be calling my son names, Simon LeGrange, or I'll teach you some manners," my father announces as he walks out of a bathroom. He stumbles and puts one hand on a chair to steady himself. "How did you find me here, Tom?"

"A kid at school said this was your office."

There are louder laughs and even a few guffaws. The laughter of Homo sapiens is not merely a spontaneous physical reaction to something that is "funny," as our observers initially concluded. I see now that humans also use laughter as a social weapon to humiliate and castigate.

"Show him your desk, Graham," a man suggests.

"Do you have business cards for that stool?"

My father glares around at them and then looks at me. "What's up? Did something happen to your mother?"

"No," I tell him. "She's fine."

"Tough luck, Graham," Simon says.

Dad throws him a scowl. "Come over here, son. Ernie, get him a cola."

"We don't serve kids."

"Just bring him a drink."

The bartender puts a Coke down in front of me and walks away shaking his head.

My father studies me and I look back at him. There's a half-finished glass of whiskey in front of him. He reaches for it and then uncurls his fingers from the glass. "This isn't my office," he tells me softly. "I just like to stop by to relax on my way home from time to time."

"Yes, sir," I say.

He winces. "Don't call me sir. I'm your dad. You're my son. You're even starting to look a little like me, back in the day when I was a young rascal." He reaches out and strokes my hair.

I blink away a tear. A particle of sawdust must have wafted into my eye.

"Hey, the Filbers are having a moment!" a fat lady a few stools away observes.

My father takes his hand away and studies my face. I think he sees the tear in my eye. "Why are you here?"

I can't tell him that in order to evaluate humanity I have decided to join its noblest cause and I need some background information. So instead I say, "I thought maybe we could walk home to dinner."

"Together, you mean?"

"Yes, sir. I mean Dad. Even if it's turkey meat loaf again."

He looks down at his drink a bit longingly and then straightens up. "I'm done, Ernie. My son and I are going to walk home to dinner together."

"Sounds like a plan," the bartender says.

Dad stands and tries to pull his jacket on, but he drops it on the floor.

"Talk about the blind leading the blind," the fat lady says out of the side of her mouth.

I bend and pick up Dad's jacket and hand it to him. He brushes sawdust off it, throws down a few dollars near his glass, and we head out of the Emerald Tavern together.

It is a cool October evening. The stores of Main Street are bustling with people. "So how's life, son?"

It's one of those very strange human questions that have no easy answer. "Better than being dead," I finally respond.

"Fair enough," he says with a smile. "Learning anything at school?"

"How to survive on Planet Earth."

"Well, that's worth the ticket, then. What about the

girls? Starting to turn your head, are they?" He grins at me. "Guess you don't have to turn very far."

"Michelle Peabody is very nice," I agree softly.

"Take it slow," he advises. "There's plenty of time."

We walk together, side by side, past the Central Grocery, Sam's Video-DVD Palace, and the Hey-Ho Dry Cleaners. His strides are longer than mine, but somehow our footsteps seem to ring out in unison. It's a surprisingly pleasant feeling.

I think for a moment of Ketchvar II, the last time I saw him on Sandoval. It was just before this mission. He's six thousand years old now, which is near the limit for the life span of a Sandovinian.

After sharing the Great Squeak, we lay in the cool mud together, savoring the gathering darkness. "Good luck on your new mission, Ketchvar."

"It will be a challenge to evaluate Homo sapiens. They are notoriously foolish and illogical."

"A challenge you're more than up to," he assured me. "We're very proud of everything you've done for the GC." He rotated his body in the ooze and said quietly, "This may be your last mission for a while."

I looked over at him. He returned my gaze from his eyestalk. "One day soon you may need to come home, to take over the Ketchvar burrow and set things in order."

"That won't be for a long time."

"Not so long, Ketchvar," he said. And the cheerful red twilight of Sandoval snapped closed into darkness.

Suddenly I hear a ferocious roar.

It's a truck, honking at me. My father pulls me back on the curb just in time. "Are you okay, son? I asked you a question, and you didn't even hear. You looked very far away. Too far to see that red light."

"I'm fine," I tell him. "I was just enjoying the walk home. What was your question, Father?"

"Who told you the Emerald Tavern was my office?"

"Jason Harbishaw. He was bullying Sally."

The light turns green but my father doesn't walk. He just stands there. "Did he put his hands on her?"

"No," I say. "He just called her some names."

Dad nods slowly, and we cross the street. We are soon walking away from the town's business district, on a tree-shaded lane. "His father was a bully, too. Not at first. We were pals. But he had a mean streak that got worse over time till he turned all mean from nose to toes."

"What happened?" I ask.

"What happened?" my father repeats. "Nothing much. Only that he robbed me blind. Made his fortune and ruined my life. Your life. All our lives." Dad spits onto the street. "Drive up there sometime and see for yourself."

"Up where?"

"Overlook Road. You won't have trouble finding it. The last house and the biggest. The air smells sweet up there. And there's a view of the town below! That's how he spends his life now. Every day he looks down at us."

"The paint factory makes a lot of money?"

"Tons."

"Why?"

My father hesitates, and then answers softly. "Some special processes they have for industrial oil-based paints. Including one developed by a fool who wasn't smart enough to get his name on the patent." He kicks a stone, and it rolls till it disappears under a parked car.

"Do these processes create toxins?"

He glances at me. "Quite the little chemist, are you? What does it matter, Tom? You never cared to hear any of this before."

"I care now," I say.

"Sure there are toxins," he finally says. "They're called VOC's—volatile organic compounds. You can't make an omelet without breaking eggs. And they've broken a lot of eggs. But let's talk about something else. Why was Jason picking on your sister?"

I decide not to tell my father about Sally's paper-writing business. "He was calling her names."

"What names?"

"Flabber. And Boulder Butt."

"No!"

"She does have a rather prominent gluteus maximus."

My father smiles. "That's not for him to judge." He squints down at me. "You have a strange way of speaking, son. Formal. Distant. I've noticed it before. Where on earth does that come from?"

"As a matter of fact, the derivation is not terrestrial," I tell him. "It's from the nebula."

"Ask a stupid question, get a nutty answer," he says, and stops walking. "Okay, lad, are you ready?"

I see that we've reached our house. "Ready for what?"

"Put on the armor, take the sword out of its sheath, and let's go face the turkey meat loaf together."

19

"Look at you two, thick as thieves," my mother says as Dad and I walk in together. "What's that about?"

"Just spending some quality time with my son," he tells her, and sniffs. "I don't smell turkey meat loaf."

"We're not having it tonight."

He flashes me a look of relief. My father has an expressive face, and he clearly enjoys sharing good news. "What are we having? Chicken? Fish? The aroma eludes me."

Tom Filber's belly is empty. I sniff the air and also draw a blank.

"Come to the table and you'll see," she says. She tilts back her head and calls, "SAAALLLLYYY, DINNER!"

We offer to help my mother serve the food, but she insists she will bring it in herself. Sally comes downstairs and the three of us sit at the table, waiting for the feast to arrive.

I skipped the turkey meat loaf last night, so this will be

my first family dinner on Planet Earth. As we wait, my dad makes polite table conversation.

"How's the cello going, Sal?" he asks.

"I hate it."

"Then why don't you stop playing it?"

"Good fatherly advice," she says. "Quit."

"I just meant that no one's forcing you to play it."

"I know what you meant."

My father looks back at her and takes a sip from his water glass. We can hear my mother fumbling around with pots and plates. Whatever she's dishing up clearly takes intricate preparation.

My father tries again. "Listen, Sal," he says. "Let's be on the same side for a minute. Do you want me to phone Jason Harbishaw and tell him to leave you alone?"

Sally glances at me. "Somebody's got a big mouth."

"Actually my mouth is average-size for boys in my age range," I tell her.

"Yeah, well maybe you should put an average-size cork in it," she suggests.

"He was only trying to help," my father explains. "He was concerned for you. And I am, too. Jason Harbishaw shouldn't be calling you insulting names."

"It's none of his business if you have a prominent gluteus maximus," I contribute.

"Say another word and I'll scream," she warns us.

"We won't talk about it further," my dad says. "But if you ever want me to put a stop to it, just . . ."

Sally tilts back her head and screeches so loud the entire room seems to start spinning. While she is in mid-yell, my mother comes in carrying a big covered platter and stands there, holding it and watching us.

Sally finally runs out of breath and falls silent, her mouth still open.

"Dinner is served," Mom announces, and sets the platter down on the table.

Oddly, I still can't smell anything. Also, I noticed that when she carried the platter in, she held one hand beneath it. Whatever is inside can't be too hot.

"Thank you for cooking, Ruth," Dad says.

"You're welcome. Enjoy."

My father reaches out and removes the cover from the platter. There is no food inside. The platter is filled with white and yellow pieces of paper of varying sizes.

"What's this?" my father asks. "A joke?"

"No joke," she tells him. She reaches into the pile of papers on the platter and randomly pulls one out. "Phone company, eighty-three dollars. We can't pay that."

"You can't let them turn off my cell phone!" Sally shrieks.

"Your mother's just a little overexcited," Dad says. "Let's go out for pizza and we'll talk about this later."

Mom gives him a look and reaches back into the pile. "Mortgage bill. Overdue. Four hundred and thirty-two dollars. We're going to lose the house."

He puts a hand gently on her arm. "Ruth, please. Don't alarm the kids. No one's going to take our house."

She pulls away violently. "STOP! I can't do it anymore,

Graham. Not on what I make at the diner. Not with you drinking it away."

"Now you know I've been looking," he tells her softly, but she cuts him off.

"We don't even have money to take your son's braces off his teeth! What kind of a man are you?"

My father stands up from the table, his face red. "Enough," he says.

"Not enough," she snaps back. "You don't even try! Damn you." She picks up her fork and throws it at him.

Dad heads for the door.

"Run away," she calls after him, and hurls a spoon. "Back to the bar. Why don't you do us a favor and stay there! COWARD!"

We hear the front door open and then slam shut.

The three of us sit at the table staring at each other over our neat place settings and the platter of bills in the center.

My mother slowly draws her hand over her face. The simple gesture seems to age her twenty years. For a moment, I can see the haggard old woman she will become, the drained, deeply lined, careworn face.

Sally stands up from her chair. "Thanks for dinner, Mom. I guess there's no dessert?"

"No," my mother whispers, "there's nothing else."

"Then I'm going upstairs," Sally says. "Why doesn't somebody just pull the lever and flush this family down the toilet?"

She walks out. I am alone with my mother.

"I don't mind the braces," I say softly.

She looks back at me, opens her napkin, dabs at the corners of her eyes two or three times, and then begins to weep into it. She's a big woman, and each time she sobs the silverware seems to rattle on the tabletop.

"It's okay." I try to soothe her in my most comforting voice.

"How is it okay?" she asks between sobs. "It's a disaster. Sally's right. I wish someone would just put us out of our misery."

I think for a second of the Gagnerian Death Ray. One gentle push, and there will be no more meals like this.

But that is a decision that must be made by Preceptors on a global level. Right now I am at this old wooden dinner table, alone with a fellow living creature in pain. It's true I am a Level-Five GC Evaluator, trained to observe impartially, but it's difficult to sit here and watch her weep into her dinner napkin.

I quickly access the consciousness of Tom Filber. *How can I make her stop crying?*

The answer comes back loud and clear from the Ragwellian Bubble. *There's nothing you can say. She's right. It's a disaster. Just leave the table before she turns on you.*

You want me to leave my mother like this? I follow up. *Isn't that kind of cold?*

She's not your mother, Snailface, he snaps. *She's my mother, remember? And she's a realist. Nothing you can say will make this better. Get out while you can.*

I am surprised by the anger in his response. He should

not be able to call me Snailface from the Ragwellian Bubble. Nor should he be able to recognize our separate identities. The part of his consciousness capable of understanding his own situation and reacting with such strong emotions should have been switched off.

Perhaps, given his extended captivity inside the bubble, he is starting to recover his identity a bit. This is a very worrisome development. I must rely on Tom Filber's practical advice for my own survival during my time on Planet Earth. If he loses his objectivity and regains elements of his own persona and will, my position will become much more difficult. *I have to try to comfort her,* I tell him.

Go ahead. Dig your own grave, he responds. *What's it to me?*

I reach across and offer my mother my dinner napkin.

She takes it and blows her nose into it.

I sit there trying to figure out what an Earthling in her position would want to hear that might be comforting. She is clearly right about the Filber family's financial plight. The pile of bills is formidable. She is also correct that my father spends his time and money at the Emerald Tavern. I saw him there an hour ago. "He still loves you very much," I finally tell her softly.

"Who?" she asks between sobs.

"My father. Your husband. I can hear it in his voice when he talks about you. He knows you had dreams that didn't all come true."

She peers up at me over the dinner napkin. "I married him at nineteen. Nineteen! I only wish I could climb back through time and slap some sense into that foolish girl."

"But you cannot," I tell her. "Time is linear. The choices we make define us, so it is wise to accept them."

She lowers the napkin and gapes at me. "What are you talking about? I swear, sometimes I barely recognize you." She takes a long breath. "How can I accept what he's done to my life? He's never tried, Tom. Do you understand that? Not once!"

"Yes, I do understand that," I tell her. "But didn't he work at the Harbishaw paint factory?" I point out. "He developed a process that made the factory profitable. Stan, the owner, stole it from him. That might break any man."

She makes a strange sound deep in her throat. At first I think she's choking, and then I realize that she's laughing bitterly. "Is that what he told you?"

"Yes."

She sits there with tears squeezing out of her red eyes, laughing and crying at the same time. "That was the only steady work he ever had."

"But he did try."

"I got that job for him," she says. "Stan gave it to Graham as a favor to me. Because Stan felt sorry for us." She twists the napkin as if she has decided to wring her tears back out of it. "Stan loved me. I could have had him. I chose your father. Because of his kind eyes, and his devilish smile, and my own immature romantic stupidity. Go up to Overlook Road sometime, and see what I could have had! Instead of this dump with bills that we can never pay."

She pulls the platter toward her and looks down at it, shaking her head. "Stan gave Graham that job, and it lasted two years before he pissed it away. And then it was gone, just like everything else that he touches. So now he's invented some grand story of stolen secret processes? Lord have mercy."

"Maybe there's some truth in what he says," I suggest softly.

My mother looks at me and her eyes narrow. "Salt in the wounds. Telling me I don't know my own husband! *I was there*. I lived through it. What do you know?" Her voice sharpens. *"What do you know about anything?"*

"Nothing, Mom," I tell her. "I am just trying to figure things out during my brief time on Planet Earth."

"Your brief time on Planet Earth is gonna be a hell on wheels if you give me any more of your attitude when I'm feeling this low!"

I do not like the way our conversation has turned. "I did not mean to give you my attitude. I would take it back if I could."

Her eyes flash. "One more sassy word out of you and you'll regret it."

I attempt to leave expeditiously, but in my haste my elbow brushes a water glass. It crashes over and breaks, spilling ice water all over my mother.

She jumps up. In a split second all of her sadness seems to have been converted to volcanic anger. "LOOK WHAT YOU'VE DONE TO MY GLASS! GET OVER HERE AND CLEAN THIS UP!"

She grabs something heavy and metallic and waves it over her head. I think it's a big serving spoon.

I decide not to clean up the broken glass. I have learned in my visit to Earth that threats of physical violence must be taken very seriously.

Mom tries to cut me off, but I put on a burst of speed, sprint to the front door, rip it open, jump down six steps, and flee.

20

I t is a cold autumn evening. Tom Filber's strong legs propel his bike steadily uphill. I need a new vantage point to consider things. I am deeply worried. My entire mission may be in jeopardy.

I steer the bike over to the side of the road and sit on a grassy knoll, looking downhill. The town of Barrisford spreads out beneath me.

There is Winthrop P. Muller High School, empty of students and looking sad in the fading light. The Hoosaguchee River twists like a silver-gray snake, slithering eastward to the distant Atlantic. I see the black thread of Beech Avenue, and I believe I can just make out a black smudge that is the roof of the Filber house. I wonder if my mother has dried her tears and contained her fury.

When I undertook this mission I had no idea that the behavior of humans would be this difficult to evaluate. How can I pass judgment on the entire human species if I cannot even assign blame in my own family? Is my father the cause of the Filbers' misery or is he a victim? Is my mother a vicious woman or a long-suffering martyr? And what of my mean and bitter big sister? How many horrible family dinners has she been forced to endure?

Here is what most concerns me. The Filber family was not studied before my insertion. The selection of a human specimen had to be completely random. If we screened possible targets it would have been impossible for us to resist selecting a human specimen whose intelligence and sensitivities were a tiny bit closer to our own. This would, of course, have invalidated all my conclusions.

But now I am very worried that in randomly selecting the Filbers, we unfortunately chose an atypically miserable and dysfunctional human family. They may not be representative of the citizens of Barrisford, or of greater humanity. If the Filbers are too far outside the norm, it will render large parts of my evaluation invalid.

Has all my work on Planet Earth been wasted? Have I needlessly dodged my mother's broom and my sister's cattle prod? Or is it possible that all the homes I see below contain families that are just as unhappy as the Filbers, albeit for different reasons? There is only one way for me to proceed—I must notify the Preceptor Supervisor of my concerns, and in the meantime continue my work here.

I get back on the bike and continue to climb upward. The evening breeze has quickened to a sharp wind that nips at my arms and face. I see a sign for Overlook Road and turn onto it.

My father was right: the air does smell sweet up here. The

houses are large and graceful and set far apart. I knew from orbital observation that there were "haves" and "have-nots" on Planet Earth, but it is only as I pedal slowly up Overlook Road that I see for myself how pronounced the disparity is between rich and poor. The Filber house is small and dilapidated. These elegant mansions are ten times as large!

Signs say: DEAD END, PATROLLED BY PRIVATE SECURITY, and KEEP OUT! The very last house on the block is by far the largest of all. It is surrounded by a fence and partially hidden by a cluster of tall trees, but I can see its grand silhouette against the purple sunset. This must be the Harbishaw estate.

Could my mother really have lived in this palace if she had chosen a different husband?

Is this mansion the specter that haunts my father's waking hours and makes him try to turn off his brain?

I steer my bike off the road, hide it behind a bush, and walk to the fence.

The house is five stories high, with turrets and terraces. I peer through the fence and see a tennis court and a swimming pool. Every bush and tree and blade of grass appears to have been recently trimmed.

A sweet smell is carried to me by the evening breeze. It is the distinctive aroma from the pomaceous fruit of the species Malus domestica—an apple tree! I spot its gnarled trunk and branches inside the fence.

It occurs to me that I know a girl who likes apples. I am an evaluator on an important mission, and I should not put myself at needless risk. Nevertheless, I am suddenly seized by the same boldness I felt when I threw the acorn. Human impulses are difficult to resist.

I climb the fence and drop down silently inside. When I land I freeze and make sure that no one has seen or heard me. My Planet Earth street smarts are on full alert.

I walk to the apple tree and scale its low branches. Leaning far out, I reach for a particularly large and ripe piece of fruit. Just as my fingers close around the apple, beautiful music begins.

I pluck it and glance at the house. A light has been switched on in a first-floor room. A woman in a blue dress sits at a piano, her fingers gliding over the keys. I can see the room clearly from my perch. It has large windows and I see shelves of books and an easel. She is all alone—she must be playing for her own gratification. Her long, flowing black hair cascades down to the gleaming piano keys.

The music she is playing is exquisitely sad. It seems to reach out from the piano and touch me, and makes me think of all the miles of cold space that separate me from dear sweet old Sandoval. *Get down from the branch, Ketchvar*, the music whispers. *Come closer and I will answer all your questions about human misery.*

I know it is risky to get any closer, but I climb down from the tree and slowly approach the house. I can see the woman in the blue dress more clearly now. Can this beauty be Stan Harbishaw's wife? She is playing the piano with deep emotion, pouring herself into the song. Her black hair flies back and forth as her fingers rise and fall.

It is not just the Filbers, the sad music says to me. *Nor does a small house or unpaid bills have anything to do with it. Look at this mansion! Look at me here, rich, talented, and beautiful, with everything I could possibly want. Don't you hear how unhappy I am?*

For a moment as she plays, her head turns toward the window and she seems to look right at me. Her eyes are half closed and her lips quiver with a powerful emotion. LISTEN! the music implores. *Can't you hear the emptiness I feel, the sense that my life is passing me by, that I have sold out my youth and dreams, and that everything I touch now rings hollow and false?*

I can almost read the name of the musical composition on the sheet music. I step even closer to the window, so that my nose is pressed to the glass. The title and the composer's name are still blurry.

I narrow Tom Filber's eyes to slits and use a Zavornian Retinal Pinch to increase my range of sight. I make out the B first, and then the smaller letters: "Beethoven Piano Sonata Opus 13—'Pathétique.'"

Then I realize that the music has stopped.

I glance back at the woman just as she stands up from the piano bench. She is now staring out the window right at me. She opens her mouth and screams.

I jerk away from the glass pane and start to run the other way, into darkness. A root reaches up out of the ground and trips me. Before I can stand back up, bright lights come on all over the grounds.

A large man exits the front door holding a baseball bat.

I crawl behind a bird feeder and lie flat, peering around

the pedestal at him. His bald head glints in the bright lights. I can tell that he once had the baby face of his son, Jason, but his features are now hard and mean. "Whoever's out there," he calls, "the cops are on their way. And I'm going to let the dogs out in a second!"

I pick up a stone and throw it as far as I can. When he looks in the direction it lands, I run the other way. Earth street smarts can come in very handy.

At any moment I expect to hear the growl of dogs, but the yard stays silent. I make it to the fence and start to climb just as a siren sounds faintly in the distance. I swing over the top, jump to the ground, find my bike behind a bush, and pedal downhill.

The human bicycle is a primitive contraption but it's silent and very fast when speeding down a steep slope. I am halfway down Overlook Road when the three police cars appear almost out of nowhere, racing up toward the mansion.

I just have time to veer sharply into a gravel driveway. My speed and momentum carry my bike off the narrow twisting drive. I fly over the handlebars, land in a particularly large thornbush, and scream.

The pain passes quickly. The three police cars disappear up the hill. I gingerly disentangle myself from the prickers and search for my bike.

21

I stow Tom Filber's old bicycle in the garage. It has gotten some new scratches and dings from my crash, but it is still quite functional.

The evening has grown so cool that I shiver as I close the garage door. It is now well past nine o'clock. I have had no dinner, and there is not likely to be much waiting for me in the house, unless I want to nibble on an old telephone bill.

I remember the apple I plucked and pull it out of my pocket. It's very tempting to take a bite, but I recall why I picked it and glance toward the Peabodys' backyard. I can't see anything, but I hear faint squeaks.

I walk toward the hedge, and sure enough, in the gathering darkness I can just make out the old swing moving back and forth. "Greetings, Michelle," I call out. "Do not be alarmed. It is not a stranger, come to harm you. It is only me, Tom Filber."

"You don't have to give me that nutty speech every

time you walk over here," she responds. "I'm not alarmed. What's up?"

It's one of those tricky human questions. I glance skyward. "The moon."

She looks back at me, and then peers up at it. "Yeah, it's a pretty one, too."

"Actually 'up' and 'down' are meaningless concepts when considering space," I point out. "But it is an attractive planetary satellite."

She asks in a soft voice, "Why don't you come on the swing and help me push."

I accept her invitation. Our toes brush as we propel the lever back and forth. Her head is tilted against the back of the swing and she is still looking up at the moon. "Can you believe that people once walked on that?"

"Only twelve of them."

"How do you know a thing like that?"

"It was a high-water mark of human achievement."

"You make it sound like we're all going down the drain," she says. Then she adds, "Can you imagine what it must have felt like to be up there? To be so far from home that you're looking down at your own planet?"

My eyes jump from the moon to the million stars in the night sky. For a moment they swirl above me, darting about like fireflies. The breeze seems to carry my father's faint voice: *Ketchvar, Ketchvar.* I hold tight to the swing and suck in a few breaths. "Yes, I can imagine how it felt," I whisper. "They must have been very brave."

She hears something in my voice and slowly lowers her gaze from the moon to my face. "Are you okay?"

"I was just thinking about my father. He's having a rough night. I sort of wish I was with him."

Michelle nods and her face seems to soften. "I can hear your parents fighting sometimes. I'm sorry. It really sucks. But I meant are *you* okay? You're bleeding."

"My epidermis just got scratched. No bones were broken and my vital organs seem intact. But thank you for your concern."

"What happened?"

"I had to dive into a thornbush to get away from the police."

Her blue eyes study me curiously. "Why were the cops chasing you?"

"I climbed a fence onto private property to pick you an apple."

She grins and then laughs. "Yeah, right."

"Here it is." I hand it to her. "It was the biggest and best-looking one on the tree."

She takes it from me and our fingers touch. "Why did you pick this?"

"Because you like apples," I tell her. "Don't you?"

"Yes, I do," she admits. She takes a bite, chews and swallows, and her pink tongue creeps out of her mouth as she licks some juice off her lips. Then she smiles at me, and her eyes glow. "Yum. Thanks. No boy's ever risked his life to pick me an apple before."

Tom Filber's adrenaline level spikes. I force it down to an acceptable level. "You're welcome," I tell her. "I was glad you showed up at the Teen Green Team meeting. I didn't think you were coming."

"Well, orchestra got canceled, and I thought I would check it out," she says. "Even though it's probably a waste of time."

"Maybe we can do some good," I tell her. "Especially if we work together. I have a few ideas."

She takes another bite of the apple and considers this. "What's gotten into you lately?"

I can't tell her that I've gotten into Tom Filber—that I crawled in through his left nostril and fused myself into his cranium using the Thromborg Technique. "What do you mean?"

"It's like you're the same guy, but somehow you've also changed. In a good way."

"Maybe I'm growing up."

"Maybe we both are," she says very seriously. She hesitates for a long moment. "Come over here for a second, Tom. I want to tell you something that's kind of private."

I slide over to her bench. Our bodies are touching, from shoulder to hip to knee.

"The other night you asked me why I sit out here alone some evenings," she whispers. "I guess it's no big secret in the neighborhood that my mom took off about a year ago. I get postcards from her. She's in San Francisco. My father works most nights. So he leaves me at home with my brother."

She breaks off for a second. It turns out that we can push the swing from the same side if we get the timing right. Our knees bend and straighten in tandem and we sail back and forth over the dark yard.

"My brother has this Goth band," she continues. "You've probably heard them practicing down in the basement. The music's pretty awful, but that's not the worst part."

"What's the worst part?" I ask.

"Some of the band members drink and smoke. And the drummer is always coming into my room and trying to put his arm around me. So I sit out here till they leave."

"I'm sorry," I tell her. What were the words she used when she commiserated with me about my dad? "That sucks."

"It's okay. I actually like sitting out here," she says. "But I don't know what I'm going to do when winter comes."

"You're always welcome in my house," I tell her.

"You have changed." She's staring at me and her blue eyes are now glowing as brightly as the silver moon high overhead. "That's the first time I ever told anyone about my brother's band and everything. Thanks for being so understanding."

"You're welcome."

"You don't always have to be so formal," she says. "I mean, we're friends, right?" She smiles at me and half closes her eyes. She's breathing a little bit harder, and I get the sense that she's waiting for me to take a decisive action.

I access the consciousness of Tom Filber. *What am I supposed to do now?*

I think she wants you to kiss her.

You think? Can't you tell for sure?

No way. No one can tell a thing like that for sure.

Aren't you a human male? Don't you understand these behavioral codes?

Hey, give me a break, I never kissed a girl before.

Why not?

Never had the chance.

What if you're wrong?

You'll probably get slapped. But I think you should go for it. This'll be my first kiss.

You mean my first kiss, I correct him.

My lips, Snailface.

I terminate the connection with the Ragwellian Bubble and take a deep breath. Michelle's eyes are now almost completely closed. Her head is tilted up toward me. She has a dreamy expression on her lovely face.

On Sandoval we do not kiss. Gastropods, after all, do not have lips. But we do have physical means of expressing affection. For example, there is the light brushing of sensory tentacles. There is no reason for a Sandovinian to be shy about initiating such an intimate moment, as long as the attraction is mutual.

I take a deep breath and lower my head toward Michelle. Her lips seem to swim away from me, and I pursue them. Finally, there is a moment of soft contact. Her blue eyes pop open, but she does not pull away. I have the distinct impression that she is kissing me back.

It is a truly wonderful moment. I did not know that the human body was capable of such sensitivity of feeling.

Unbidden, Tom Filber makes an excited suggestion from the Ragwellian Bubble: *Go for some tongue action.*

I hesitate for a second. *Why? This is so pleasant.*

It will get even hotter! Go for it. She expects it! She's waiting for it!

He is, after all, a human, and far more familiar with the habits of Earthlings than I am. I lift my tongue and gently lick the outside of her lower lip.

Michelle jerks away. "What are you doing?"

"Nothing," I tell her.

She stands up. "It's really late. And cold. I've gotta go." She jumps down from the swing and hurries off through the darkness toward her house.

22

Subject: How to Whistle with Broken Glass

Revered Galactic Confederation Elders. Ketchvar here, banging out a message on Tom Filber's laptop, in a bit of a panic. I'm very concerned about my mission.

Taking on a human body is increasingly difficult to manage. I find myself susceptible to primitive and powerful urges and impulses. This morning I threw an acorn at a fellow human's head, and I was glad that it hit him! Now, when I should be concentrating on this urgent GC communication, I find myself stopping every fifteen seconds to gaze across at Michelle Peabody's dark window.

Is she lying awake? Is she furious at me for kissing her? Does she occasionally glance back at my window?

Esteemed Preceptors, there seems to be a serious problem with the Ragwellian Bubble. Tom Filber is beginning to recover his identity and elements of his free will. He has even found a way to communicate with me of his own volition!

How can I expect to survive on Planet Earth without being able to trust the advice of a native? If he recovers more of his free will, he may actively rebel! He might use his position of adviser to give me the worst possible advice.

I glance across at Michelle's window. Why did she run away like that? Was she disgusted? Or merely surprised?

Did Tom Filber tell me to go for some tongue action out of ignorance? He had, after all, never kissed a girl before. Or was he intentionally sabotaging my romantic moment? Is he already unreliable? Do I have an enemy inside my own cranium?

Revered Elders, I fear we may have randomly selected a family that is not representative of the human condition. I suggest a team of GC analysts immediately go to work on the question of whether all human families are this miserable and dysfunctional, or if I had the bad luck to hop off our spaceship into a loony bin of a household.

How can I condemn species Homo sapiens because of a mean sister and a violent mother, if there are nice families up and down the block? On the other hand, Michelle Peabody is a lovely girl but her mother ran out on her, her father is irresponsible, and her brother the Goth band manager doesn't sound very nice.

Her bedroom curtain flutters and I glance over. For a moment I think I can see the outline of her face. I raise my right hand and give her a tentative wave. There is no reaction. I attempt a Retinal Pinch, but I cannot pierce the darkness of her room, and then she is gone.

Esteemed Elders, I have one more urgent and very personal concern.

I have felt the presence of my father, Ketchvar II, trying to contact me from Sandoval. He may have thrown his essence Earthward in a desperate Interstellar Transference.

I am extremely worried about him.

He would have attempted such hazardous contact only if he were lost, in pain, or dying. Sandovinians of extreme age sometimes leave their burrows and wander about in the ooze. They can freeze to death or sink so far down that the mud congeals over them and they asphyxiate.

Can you please check and see if my father is missing from the Ketchvar burrow?

During my last visit home, when he wished me well on this mission, he intimated that he might be growing feeble. My mind was already on Planet Earth and this evaluation. I should have paid more attention to what he was trying to tell me.

Revered Elders, he has been a good father and since I am now trapped in Barrisford, inside a human body, on a vitally important GC mission, I must depend on your assistance. Please contact me as soon as you get any word of his condition.

I will keep my Emergency Contact Wibbler on through the night, or you can send me a message on Tom's laptop. Thank you! I am counting on your kind help!

The night breeze stirs a branch that brushes my window, and I hear my father's very faint voice crying, *Ketchvar, where are you? I'm lost in darkness!*

I stop typing and sit very still. Then I stand and bolt out of Tom Filber's room, down the steps, and out into the cold New Jersey night.

23

I sprint to the backyard and find a spot beneath the crab apple tree. I sink to the ground, my back against the trunk, my eyes upturned to the branches and leaves.

I force my worries away and wipe my mind blank. All I hear now are the buzzing of night insects and the rustle of the leaves above my head. The cold breeze blows through me. I reach down deep into myself for the very essence of Ketchvar, and liberate myself.

Gone are the physical limitations of a boy who needs a dinged-up bicycle to escape the police. Also gone for the moment are earthly concerns like an overly ambitious kiss bestowed on a friendly neighbor.

I float up through space. I do not see our spaceship, but I do not pause to look for it. Instead, I hurl myself homeward. Stars cartwheel and somersault, and then merge into a chalky streak traced over a slate black background of emptiness.

Two scarlet pinpricks emerge in the distance. The twin suns of Sandoval.

I float down. It is pitch-dark. The Great Squeak has ended and Sandovinians are in their burrows.

I find Mud Cluster Seven in the Chigaboid Quadrant.

There is a commotion in the Ketchvar burrow. I see old friends and family members, looking worried. Search parties are setting out, slithering through the cold night ooze and lifting off on silver floaters.

I wish I were there, I should be there directing the search! But I can only join them in spirit. My astral presence follows my relatives through the ooze, listening as they call out to my father.

I soar with another search party over Sandoval's surface on a silver floater, while scanners probe the cool muck for Ketchvar II's unique chemical fingerprint.

No one finds him. No search party hears him. No scanner senses him.

I had forgotten how silent Sandoval is at night: as dark and silent as death itself.

I am filled with dread and regret. I have been so busy with my GC business that I have visited home rarely in the past thousand years. Even when I did return, I did not heed the warning signs.

I float high over the dark orb of Sandoval. I cannot speak, but risk an interstellar thought plea: *Father, I'm sorry. I should not have left you.*

A weak voice floats up from the inky blackness. *Ketchvar, Ketchvar, I am lost.*

Describe your surroundings, Father. Are you stuck in clay? Is the mud salty? Is it wet or dry? Have you corkscrewed so far down that the ooze is congealing?

I must already be dead, my son. It is your burrow now.

No, Father. Search parties are looking for you. There's still time. I'm sorry I'm not there.

Don't blame yourself, Ketchvar. You were doing important work.

What could be more important than taking care of my own father?

It's so dark here. I do not fear death, but I fear this dark and the biting cold.

Hold on. They'll find you!

I hear a strange sound—a bitter laugh. Can it be the mocking bray of death itself, interposing itself between father and son?

The twin suns of Sandoval recede. The stars bubble and steam around me like cosmic soup.

I hurtle back through space. There is Planet Earth. North America. Barrisford. The crab apple tree in the Filbers' backyard.

The laugh rings out again. It's brutal and derisive. It seems to say: *I warned you. Now you'll pay for messing with me!* The laugh saws through the cold night air and vibrates. Not a laugh—bad cello music!

I am seated on the patchy grass of the Filber backyard, drenched in my own sweat even though the night is quite cold.

My sister is up in her room, practicing. She must have left her window open. The dissonant cello music leaps from her windowsill and takes wing like a bat. It flutters around the backyard and lands on my shoulder.

I pull away from it, but I can't shake it off. The bat bares its sharp teeth at me.

You made a mistake, it hisses at me. *I warned you. Now you will pay!*

24

I sprint back up the stairs to my room. My door is wide open.

Tom Filber's laptop glows—I recall that I left it on when I ran outside.

An intruder has been in my room messing with it! Someone has read my message to the revered GC Elders! The files labeled "Old Hip-Hop Songs That Sucked" and "How to Sauté a Skunk" have been opened.

My fingers fly across the keyboard as I try to assess the damage. Oh no! Not that! Anything but that! The intruder has forwarded my messages to several different blogs that my schoolmates read!

The whole world will now know about my mission!

My cover is blown! My schoolmates will tell their parents who will immediately alert state and national authorities that an alien presence is hiding in their midst.

The army will come rolling up Beech Avenue to find and destroy me.

I glance out the window. The street is dark and quiet. There are no jeeps or tanks yet.

It is late in the evening. Perhaps no one has seen the blog postings yet. There may still be time to undo the damage.

No, several of my fellow students have already read my letters, and their comments are now popping up on our school message board in response. No one seems to believe my story. The comments are sarcastic:

"Since the Galactic Confederation picked our high school to decide the future of the human race, do you think they could give the girls' softball team new uniforms?"

"His father's a boozer and it sounds like he must be smoking some potent Sandovinian weed."

"Can somebody please make my chemistry teacher disappear with a Flindarian Lapse?"

More and more comments pop up, and as I read them Tom Filber's room spins around me. The professional wrestlers pictured on the walls reach out to scoop me up and body-slam me. The singers open their mouths wide and spew violent hip-hop.

Tom Filber's favorite computer game, Galactic Warrior, pops onto the screen and the human hunters join together to blow an alien to bits.

I am hyperventilating wildly. My limbs tremble. I feel an urge to run, to get out, to flee! This must be what humans call a panic attack.

The damage is irreversible! Details of my secret mission have not only been posted, but they have been read. The news is now spreading in a ripple effect. No force in the universe can contain it. The first fools to read my letters may be laughing, but some Earthling with a few brains will understand the truth.

I wrap my arms around myself and try to slow my heartbeat. Cardiac arrest will not solve my problems.

I wrote about how the humans are the laughingstock of the galaxy. They will not take kindly to that portrayal.

I revealed GC projections that they are within a decade of destroying themselves. Earthlings will not be able to handle such dire predictions.

I recorded critical assessments of the shallowness of their top artists and scientists.

I also described some of my experiences during my brief visit to Planet Earth.

I revealed that I was beaten on the way to school.

I confessed to throwing an acorn at a bully's head.

I wrote of my feelings for Michelle Peabody, and mentioned our kiss.

No, I cannot possibly stay here. My mission has become untenable and my life is in danger. The only thing that makes sense now is immediate extraction.

I pull out the package of sugar doughnuts. My wibbler is switched on. I hail the spaceship.

No answer.

I fight to stay calm. There are two logical reasons for this. First, intense solar flare-ups can disrupt even decimeter band transmissions. I will have to keep trying. No doubt the solar storm will be short-lived, and in an hour or so I will get through to the Preceptor Supervisor.

There is another possibility why the spaceship is not answering my summons. When I threw my essence into space to get news of my father, I noticed that my spaceship was not in its orbit. An emergency may have broken out on a nearby Confederation world. When I began this mission, there was fear of an outbreak of microtic plague on Bubos VII. If plague hit that crowded planet, my spaceship may have been dispatched for an emergency rescue mission.

They would not leave me alone on Planet Earth for very long. At most, I may be stranded here for a few days. But I will be at the mercy of Earthlings who now know exactly who I am and why I am in their midst.

Something dark and ominous squeezes in under my door and flutters around Tom Filber's bedroom. *Now your jugular is exposed,* the bat hisses, its red eyes ablaze. *You have no place to hide.*

Panic gives way to anger. I stand up, rip open my door, and storm across the hallway. I burst into Sally's room.

She is seated in her chair by the open window, pulling her bow vigorously back and forth as if she is trying to saw the cello in half. "Did you forget how to knock?" she asks without looking up.

I am a civilized Sandovinian and a trained GC evaluator, but it takes all my willpower to resist the violent impulse to run over there and put my foot through her cello. I stand frozen, struggling with myself, so furious that I cannot move or speak.

Sally stops playing and glances up at me. "Do you mind? I'm trying to practice."

"Why?" I whisper.

"Why what?"

"Why did you do it?"

"I warned you to stay out of my business."

"I didn't do anything to you to deserve this," I say, walking closer to her.

"Take one more step and I'll scream for Mom," she threatens. "Go ahead and try me. See what happens. *One more step and you'll regret it*. She's already super pissed off at you."

I stop walking and stand with my hands on my hips. "Foolish, pathetic Earthling. You have no idea of the damage you've caused," I tell her. "Not just to me, but to my mission, and potentially to your entire species. I was trying to be charitable, but you've taken that last chance for your brothers and sisters away. Shame on you."

"Fine. Shame on me," she says. "Terminate my species and please shut my door on your way out."

25

The police car rattles up the unpaved road and stops near me.

I am sitting at the edge of the turtle pond in Beaverdale Park. I thought I was well concealed between two bushes, but Sergeant Collins must have sharp eyes. He gets out of the driver's side with a serious look on his face.

So they have found me. Now they will take me to the police station and then to an army post and then probably to a top-secret CIA prison-lab where they will try to separate me from the body of Tom Filber. Their top scientists will run tests on me. They will torture me for information about the Confederation.

Sergeant Collins is wearing a gun on his belt. He has no doubt already called in my location and radioed for support. There is nothing I can do. I raise my hands.

"What are you doing, Filber?"

"I surrender."

"Put your arms down and don't give me any lip or you'll regret it," he snaps.

I lower my arms.

"What are you doing here?"

"Watching turtles."

He glances toward the pond. Then back at me. "There's a little thing called school on weekdays. Did you forget about that?"

"No, sir. I was not feeling well."

"You look okay now. Maybe watching the turtles improved your health."

"Yes, I am starting to feel a little better."

"Then let's get you to school," he says. "I just happen to be heading in that direction. Get in."

Perhaps this is a clever way of taking me into custody. I ride next to him in the front seat, expecting him to pull out his gun or clamp handcuffs on my wrists at any moment. But he drives me up the hill toward school. "How's your dad?"

"On a trip," I tell him.

"Where?"

"I'm not sure."

"You don't know where your own dad is?"

I think of Ketchvar II and the search parties scouring the mud of Sandoval. "No, sir."

"When's he getting back?"

"I'm not sure."

"That's pretty screwed up."

I manage a nod.

"He's not a bad man, your father," Sergeant Collins says.

"We used to play football together. Had an undefeated team senior year. Did he ever tell you about those days?"

"No, sir."

"He was a hell of a player. Smart, too. Voted 'most likely to succeed.' When he went away to college I never thought he'd come back here. But he had a thing for your mom. Hell, half the boys in town did." Sergeant Collins steers his car to a stop in front of our school. "You worried about him?"

"A bit."

"I figured it wasn't just the turtles. He'll come back. He hasn't had an easy time of it, but he's not going to walk out on his family."

"Thank you," I say. "I mean, for the ride."

"Don't let me catch you playing hooky again," he tells me. "Now git in that door and learn something."

I walk hesitantly through the front door.

Classes are changing. The security guard is momentarily distracted. I slip by him and plunge into the crowded hallway.

I instantly become the center of attention.

Everyone watches me. Nobody says anything.

The entire Winthrop P. Muller student body seems to be stunned into a kind of collective shock. Their "Alien" has turned out to be a real alien! Now he is in their midst. They are nervously digesting the information, trying to figure out what to do next.

I hear whispers. I feel stares.

Keep a low profile, I tell myself. Skulk. The school day

is already half over. I just have to make it through three more periods. My wibbler is on. The spaceship will return from Bubos VII any moment. The sympathetic voice of the Preceptor Supervisor will reach out to me. "Sorry, Ketchvar. The plague has been averted. Now we can get you out of this mess." He will already have an extraction strategy plotted.

I turn into a hallway and run into Michelle Peabody. When she sees me she stops walking. I can tell from the way her blue eyes sharpen that she read my letters off the Internet. She does not look pleased that the entire school now knows that we kissed and I went for some "tongue action."

I open my mouth to try to explain, but she turns her back on me and hurries away.

I will have to find a better time to apologize to her. This is a day when I am focused on just surviving.

I am a few minutes late for gym class. The other boys are already on the field. I put on shorts and a T-shirt and hurry out.

Today we are playing flag football. Mr. Curtis, our instructor, paces the sideline shouting helpful advice.

"Thanks for joining us, Filber. Better late than never. That's the ugliest-looking pass I've seen in fifteen years! Can't you throw a spiral? Do you even know what a spiral is?"

Yes, I am very familiar with the shape. Our galaxy is a spiral. Soon I will be safe on a spaceship speeding homeward through its long and glowing concentric arms.

Flag football ends. The locker room is unsupervised. My earth street smarts tell me it is a dangerous place. I stay outside in the hall, by the water fountain, and let everyone else enter first. After a dozen sips of cold water I tiptoe in.

I wait for them all to finish showering before I take my turn. I am rinsing soap off my arms when I hear footsteps. Scott and Zitface appear. They are fully dressed. There is no reason they should be heading back to the shower. "Hi, Tom. How's everything with the Galactic Confederation?" Zitface asks in a friendly voice.

I look back at him. "Pretty good."

"Any word from your father in the red ooze?" Scott asks.

"No, but thank you for asking."

"You're welcome," he says. Then he steps toward me. "Don't scream," he mutters. "That will make it worse." He has a mean look on his face. I have seen it before, when he made me eat dirt.

I access the consciousness of Tom Filber. *What's my way out of here?*

You got into this, you get out, he says.

If they break my leg, they break yours, I remind him.

Yeah, but I won't feel it in this bubble.

I'll leave one day soon, and you'll spend the rest of your life limping around.

Turn on the hot water and run out through the back exit, he advises quickly.

I turn the hot water on full blast, and Scott jumps back with a curse. I dart to the spigot on the opposite side and turn that shower on hot also. A wall of steaming spray now separates me from Scott and Zitface. While they're trying to shut the scalding water off, I sprint out the back exit.

Two other boys are waiting for me there in ambush. They catch me. I struggle but there is no escape.

I try to scream for help but one of them punches me in the stomach. Suddenly my lungs are empty. I gasp so hard there are tears in my eyes.

Scott and Zitface run up. I struggle but they carry me to a corner of the locker room. All the other boys have left. They pin me on my back to a bench.

Scott stands above me. "Let's get two things straight," he says to me. "First, the only thing that's saving you right now is that you didn't mention my name. But you did write about being roughed up on the way to school. That's not information to be released. You understand that, you little weirdo?"

I nod. "No one on Earth was supposed to read those letters. My sister came into my room and . . ."

He grabs my right ear and pulls it so hard I'm afraid it will come off. "Do you understand or not?"

"Yes."

"Second, I'm sure Michelle won't go within smelling distance of you anymore, but you're gonna leave her alone. She's mine. No more swinging. No more kisses." He draws back his fist. "You got that?"

"Yes."

Instead of punching me, he slaps me in the face so hard my ears ring and my nose starts to bleed.

He turns to the others. "He's a snail creature. He likes being inside a shell. Get that garbage can over here."

They drag over a tall, cylindrical garbage can, partially filled with trash. I struggle, but they force my arms to my sides and wedge me into it feetfirst. They tip the can over and roll me to the darkest corner of the room.

"Find his clothes," Scott commands. "Check his pockets. See if there's a package of sugar doughnuts."

A second later I hear someone say, "Here it is!"

"Hey, Alien, isn't this your emergency communication device?" Scott asks, holding it in front of my face. "Let's see you use it."

They wedge the package of sugar doughnuts into my mouth. The plastic breaks and I choke and gag on powdered sugar.

But the wibbler is on! I can feel its decimeter pulse. I cry out, "Preceptor, I need help." My voice sounds high-pitched and feeble.

Scott and the other boys roar with laughter. "Do it again."

"It's Ketchvar. My life is in grave danger. I request immediate extraction!"

"Your life will be in danger if you tell anybody who did this to you," Scott promises.

They take my T-shirt and drape it over my face so that I cannot see and have trouble breathing.

I hear the gang walk away.

I am alone. I try to escape, but I cannot free my arms or legs. The stench from the garbage can is putrid.

My only hope is the wibbler. It is lying on the floor, a few inches from my chin, encased in stale doughnut. I tilt my head toward it. "Preceptor, this is an emergency. At least tell me when I can expect help. Come in, PLEASE . . ."

There is no answer. The only sound is the steady drip, drip, drip of water from the shower room.

26

Tom, I'll be honest, I don't believe you," Miss Schroeder tells me. "Maybe the boys who attacked you did grab you from behind and put a shirt over your head. But I think you know who they were. And I wish you'd trust us enough to tell the principal, or the police, or at least me."

I shrug. School is over. This is the last interrogation I will have to face. As soon as she allows me to leave, I'll be out the door and down the block. I'll wibble the spaceship every hour till they return. Soon the pain and humiliation of being stuffed naked into a garbage can will be a distant memory as I zoom homeward at a thousand light-years per second.

"I read your short stories," she says. "I understand your sister posted them on the Net without your permission. That was mean of her." She waits. "Is there anything you want to tell me about them?"

"They weren't short stories," I finally respond. "They were letters."

"Whatever they were, I have to ask you some questions about them. I know this isn't the first time you've been bullied. Right?"

I count the dust streaks on her window. It should be washed more regularly.

"It would only be natural to try to hit back at people who hurt you."

"Not for me," I tell her truthfully. I am a peaceful member of a four-million-year-old civilization. Sandoval was a founding member of the Galactic Confederation and helped write pacifism into its charter.

"You wrote about some kind of death ray." She glances down at her notes. "A Gagnerian Death Ray." She gives me a little smile. "It sounds ominous. You don't actually have one?"

I hold out my open palms for inspection. "No death rays. None in my pockets. None up my sleeves."

"Ever thought of trying to get one?"

"Never."

She hesitates a long beat. She is a kind woman and she knows her next question may hurt me. Finally she asks, "How about up on your spaceship?"

Her little office suddenly feels cold. I open my mouth to answer and then close it again.

"That's the whole point of your mission, isn't it?" she probes softly. "To evaluate, and if we don't measure up, to destroy? I agree with a lot of what you wrote. The human race can be very ugly. I see it every day in this office. There is a lot of pain. We are destroying our planet and another race might well do better. Are you really tempted to take that decision into your own hands?"

I look back into her large and compassionate brown eyes and whisper, "Miss Schroeder, you don't have to worry about me."

"I'm not worried about you," she says. "I'm worried for you." She leans forward and asks gently, "Tom, do you know what an empowerment fantasy is?"

I shiver even though sunlight is streaming through the dusty window. "I'm not sure."

She should not be doing this to me. She is an evaluator, not a torturer. Her job is to listen, not to eviscerate. Apparently, even the kindest Earthlings have the urge to destroy. I know who I am, thank you very much. Ketchvar III, GC Evaluator, from the Chigaboid Quadrant. And who are you, madam, to question me this way? A member of a species that the entire galaxy finds hilarious.

"Sometimes when we're threatened, we make up a little story about ourselves that makes us feel better and safer and stronger," she explains. "There's nothing wrong with that. As long as we know deep down that it's just a story."

I glance down at my track shoes. There is mud on the sides from my visit to the turtle pond. I move my head without looking up. I am not nodding to acknowledge that she is right. My eyes are just following the pattern of mud on the shoes.

"You have a very rich imagination," she continues.

"That's a marvelous thing. I know those letters you wrote were not supposed to be shown to anyone. You have a right to write anything you want in private. A favorite writer of mine, Kafka, wrote a famous story about being turned into a cockroach. We're talking about stories, right?"

"Yes," I whisper back. "Just stories. Can I go now?"

"I think we should talk regularly," she says. "If you ever feel like you're going to hurt yourself or anyone else, you have to come to me right away. Okay?"

"Okay."

She holds out her hand and smiles. "Promise?"

We shake. "I promise."

27

"Behold, the end of the end, the last of their kind," Mr. Stringfellow says. He is manipulating the controls of an old slide projector.

I do not want to be in this room. The only reason I am here is that Miss Schroeder insisted on walking me down to this club after we left her office. "I think it's terrific that you joined," she said. "I'm proud of you."

She escorted me right to the door and watched me enter. So now I am sitting here with Fruit Bat and Tree Boy, trapped in Mr. Stringfellow's apocalyptic slide show.

On the screen, I see a small sandy-colored bird with orange legs and a black ring around the base of its neck. "Piping plovers. Cute, aren't they?" the old science teacher asks. "When the chicks walk, they look like little windup toys. There used to be millions of them up and down the Atlantic coast." He pauses to suck in a breath of oxygen. "Then their feathers became popular in hats. Now we're down to fewer than two thousand pairs. Soon they'll be gone."

Everyone is focused on the screen. I would like to be gone from this club meeting. I wonder if I could sneak out the door. Unfortunately it is in the front of the room and Mr. Stringfellow keeps it closed.

A new slide clicks on. "The northern bog turtle," he says, smiling as if recognizing an amusing old friend. "Four inches long. Distinctive orange and yellow blotches on either side of its head. A slow walker, also slow to reproduce, and highly sensitive to the slightest changes in its environment. Unfortunately, the places it likes to live are places that people have decided to drain and move into. Cat Girl and Fruit Bat, keep a sharp eye out for bog turtles in the Swamouth Swamp. If you see one, photograph it but don't pick it up. One of the most powerful tools we have to stop overdevelopment is to show that an endangered species lives right in our midst."

Hello, I am right in your midst, I am thinking. I was just stuffed into a garbage can. Put me up on the screen, Mr. Stringfellow. I am far more threatened than the piping plover or the bog turtle.

There are still four thousand piping plovers but I am, in fact, the only one of my kind on Planet Earth. My spaceship is far away. My human host is rebelling. My neighbor hates me because I went for tongue action. My father is missing, somewhere in the red ooze a million light-years away. And my sanity has just been questioned. Much as I am sympathetic to the plight of piping coastal birds and bog turtles, right now I can only think about Ketch-var III.

"Let's turn to a lovely little fish," Stringfellow says, clicking a new slide on the screen. "The brown speckled mucker."

I stare at it and feel a jolt of surprise and recognition. I have seen this creature before!

"Three inches long. With sequinlike scales on its belly. Once plentiful in the rivers and streams of New Jersey. Now extremely threatened."

I recall my bike trip to the banks of the Hoosaguchee. Just before I went on my Flindarian Lapse, I spotted a fish much like this one. I remember that as it swam in the water, its stomach flashed a beam of light at me. That must have been the sequinlike scales.

But even if this is true, I do not care today. My elbows are raw where skin was rubbed off when I was stuffed into the garbage can. I feel unmoored. Cut loose. My anxiety level is spiking. Sweat is beading across my forehead. I need to get out the door.

Mr. Stringfellow turns the lights on. He is also looking rather endangered. Now that the lights are on, I see that he is trembling more than usual, and his face has a waxlike pallor. "End of slide show, time for progress reports," he rasps. "Ralph and Green Boy, how's it going in Beaverdale Park?"

The thin boy who favors the color green says, "We got a map of the park. We've divided it up into four zones: the meadow, the ball fields, the turtle pond, and the forest.

We're concentrating on the forest, counting up the old-growth trees, checking their condition."

"We're climbing them," Ralph adds. "Some of them are really hard to get up because the branches are so high."

"Persevere," Mr. Stringfellow says. "A tree census is a good first step. Cat Girl and Fruit Bat, what of the swamp?"

"We've made a list of the animals and insects we've seen there," Sue Ellen says. "There were a few really pretty butterflies. And we did see some cats."

"They looked wild and hungry," Fruit Bat adds.

"Beware the feral cat," Mr. Stringfellow advises. Then he turns to me. "What's happening in the Hoosaguchee River these days?"

"I don't know," I tell him.

He looks disappointed. "You and your friend from the orchestra haven't visited yet?"

"She's not my friend," I mutter. "She's not part of this club." I don't add that I'm positive Michelle will never come to a club meeting again, or any activity that I'm associated with.

Ralph and Tree Boy must have read my letters on the Internet. One of them makes a kissing sound and the other one laughs.

"You could start the project on your own," Mr. Stringfellow suggests.

I am starting to hyperventilate. My chest feels tight, as if my shirt is shrinking around my body, slowly constricting me like a snake. I need to get out of this school with its stinky garbage cans and its torturing therapists and its nutty old science teachers. I need to be free to try to contact my spaceship. I want to go home, to my safe and normal world. "I have a lot of other things going on right now," I tell him.

"It's easy to be distracted," he agrees. "That's why we must redouble our efforts here. We must make saving the earth our number one priority."

"I can't do that." I stand up.

Mr. Stringfellow moves between the door and me. "Why not?" His waxy face is challenging. His eyes bore into mine.

Get out of my way, Earthling. Your single-minded cause is not my cause. Your blighted planet is not my planet. Sandoval is pristine. Now let me go! "Because right now I need to take care of myself," I tell him.

"We all have our problems. I have a few of my own these days." He coughs and sucks oxygen. "Here's the deal. If I give a damn, you have to give a damn. The mark of a man is how he triumphs over his personal problems to accomplish something that is truly important."

I look back at him. The mark of a GC evaluator is that he accurately reads a situation and reports back on what should be done. "I respect you, but you are wrong. It is not my earth and I do not need to make my mark as a man."

"What the heck does that mean?" he asks.

Someone whispers, "Alien." I think it's Sue Ellen.

I try to get around Mr. Stringfellow. He is slow and connected to an oxygen canister but somehow he cuts me off.

"Stay," he says. "I can tell you belong here."

"You know nothing about me. We have less in common than an elephant and a sea sponge. Get out of my way. I just want to go home."

He reaches out a trembling hand to try to stop me, but I push around him. For a moment I'm afraid he may fall over, but he manages to grab the metal rod that juts up from his oxygen tank.

I yank the door open. Just as I'm leaving I hear him say, "Fool. Don't you know you are home?"

28

A day of fear gives way to a night of anxiety.

I am trying very hard not to think about something. It keeps circling back toward me, like a creature in a nightmare. I have shut it up in the back closet in the most remote corner of Tom Filber's mind. But the human brain is not good at locking nagging worries away. I can hear its wings fluttering against the closet door. I try to forget about it by focusing on my other problems.

I have still not received any message from the Preceptor. Did something happen to the spaceship? Could an asteroid have struck it? Such accidents do occur, even to the most sophisticated interstellar craft.

I try three times to throw my mind skyward in a Flindarian Lapse to search for the spaceship and check on my father, but I cannot achieve separation. In order to liberate my essence I need to wipe my mind blank. I am ashamed to admit it, but after all my years of advanced GC training, I cannot muster the discipline.

The routine of day-to-day life is supposed to distract humans from their worst fears. But the Filber home provides no relief. Everything is unsettled at 330 Beech Avenue, as if all the rules have suddenly been tossed out the window.

There is no dinner. Sally and I have to fend for ourselves. My mother is too upset about my father to cook anything. One minute she is cursing him and the next she is afraid that she may have driven him away for good. She paces from room to room. She snaps at us and then breaks off in mid-sentence. Her eyes are red and pensive.

It's best to avoid her. I find a small bag of potato chips and eat it on the back porch, looking up at the night sky. It is a clear, dark night, and the stars spill across the heavens like gold coins that have been dumped out of a chest. The familiar constellations of the galaxy should calm me. Instead, they unsettle me.

Somewhere up there my father has either emerged from the ooze or been declared dead. I have no way of contacting him or finding out about his condition.

I have wrapped the sugar doughnut with my wibbler in tinfoil. I keep it near me at all times. Occasionally I whisper into it, "Come in. This is Ketchvar. Can anyone read me?"

Then I wait. The only reply I get is the buzz of night insects from our backyard.

The thing I am trying not to think about is, in its own way, even more distressing than my father's predicament, or the spaceship's absence. Now that I am on the back porch, alone, I am tempted to release it from the closet and take it on. I recall Mr. Stringfellow's last words to me, as I fled his club: "Fool. Don't you know you are home?"

No, I tell myself, keep the closet locked.

Tom Filber is enjoying my predicament. His disembodied voice filters out of the Ragwellian Bubble and mocks me. *So you wanted to be human? This is what you get for stealing my body, you gastropod geek. Being a fourteen-year-old is no day at the beach. You've messed everything up, and it's only going to get worse. Michelle hates your guts. The kids in school threw you out like garbage. Why don't you go back to Sandoval and let me try to pick up the pieces? Oh yeah, I forgot, your ride left without you. Tough luck. You're just as trapped as I am!*

You cannot talk to me that way, I tell him. *You have no willpower.*

I have plenty of willpower. I'm going to find a way out of here and take back what's mine.

One more word out of you and I will move you from the parietal lobe to the colon, I threaten him. *Be silent!*

"Are you talking to me?" my mother asks. She has walked onto the porch.

"No," I tell her. "I was talking to the insects. They make so much noise I can't think."

"That's what insects do at night," she says. Her eyes move to the bag of potato chips I have almost emptied. I'm afraid she is going to yell at me for eating chips on the porch. But instead she offers me a banana. "Here, at least eat something healthy."

I take the banana. "Thanks."

She stands looking off into the darkness of the backyard. She is not gazing up at the stars. She is staring at the empty driveway. My father's old car is not there. "Where is that good-for-nothing? He wasn't at the bar all day. None of his friends have seen him. He's never taken off like this."

"He will come home soon," I tell her, repeating what Sergeant Collins said. But I am thinking, Why would he? You have driven him away with your temper and your insults. He is a good man, but he has had enough. He is probably five hundred miles away by now.

"I hope he doesn't come back," she says. "We'll be better off without him in the long run." But there is a hollowness in her voice when she says it, and I notice that her red eyes never stray for long from the empty driveway.

"The human condition is a difficult one," I tell her. "The stresses and uncertainties are debilitating."

She peers down at me. "You are the strangest boy. But we didn't exactly make it easy for you." She walks over and sits down next to me on an old sofa. "I got a call from school," she says. "They said you'd been in some trouble."

"It was no big deal."

"Some kids roughed you up?"

"It's okay."

"No, it's not okay. Who was it? I'll call their parents."

"You will just make things worse for me."

I am afraid she is going to insist, but instead she asks, "How's the banana?"

"Not bad."

She puts her right hand on my shoulder. It is the same hand she uses to swing a broom at me, so the tender gesture isn't completely convincing. "If you want to fight your own battles, I'll let you fight them."

"I am not a fighter," I tell her. "I believe in peace." It is the guiding principle of the civilized universe. It has led Sandoval to millions of years of happiness and prosperity.

"Peace will not protect you," she says.

"It has more power than you know."

She looks back at me. "Sometimes it's scary how much you remind me of your father when he was young. There was a time when I actually believed his silliness."

I look up at the constellations and say softly, "You can believe this. There are wonderful things out there that you know nothing about."

Her hand grips my shoulder harder. "Tom, listen to me. If I've learned anything from slaving away for fifteen years in a greasy diner and raising two kids on next to nothing, it's that you can't run away and hide," she says. "You can't pretend some wonderful bolt from the blue is suddenly going to strike that will turn everything around. That's a fool's escape." She glances at the empty driveway and her face hardens. "Be a man and face the facts. It's an ugly world but you have to take it for what it is. If you look for an easy way out in a pipe dream or an empty beer glass, you'll only be making it worse for yourself and those who love you."

She stands up from the sofa and slowly walks off the porch. The screen door swings shut behind her. I know she was trying to be helpful by warning me not to turn out like my father, but her words had an unintended effect. They opened the closet door and released the creature.

29

It is two in the morning. The house is silent. My mother has finally stopped pacing and gone to sleep.

I am sitting at Tom Filber's desk, feverishly scanning Web site after Web site. Occasionally I pause for a sip of water and I glance out at Michelle Peabody's dark window. She has no doubt also gone to sleep. The entire town of Barrisford is snoring away. I am the only one who is awake, the only one who is different. Or am I?

"Fool. Don't you know you are home?" Mr. Stringfellow demanded. Could he be right?

"You can't pretend some wonderful bolt from the blue is suddenly going to strike that will turn everything around," my mother said. "That's a fool's escape." Is that what I'm trying to do?

"Sometimes when we're threatened, we make up a little story about ourselves that makes us feel better and safer and stronger," Miss Schroeder said. "There's nothing wrong with that. As long as we know deep down that it's just a story." Could she know me better than I know myself? Is it possible that I really am Tom Filber, a miserable boy, unappreciated and abused at home and picked on at school, who dreamed up a fantasy to make myself feel better?

On one level, I know this can't be true. I am absolutely certain that I am Ketchvar III from Sandoval. I have a lifetime's worth of memories to prove it. As I sit here at Tom Filber's desk, I can picture hundreds of worlds that I visited on different missions. I can recall my happy childhood on Sandoval, and retrace my GC training from entry-level cadet to level-five evaluator. And I can remember the exact second when I left my safe shell behind and slithered out across the floor of the spaceship to take possession of Tom Filber's body.

But here's the thing that worries me. This is the conundrum that is keeping me up long into the night, twisting my stomach tighter and tighter. Behold the monster, finally let out of the closet and now flapping around Tom Filber's bedroom with dark wings and blazing eyes: I can't prove any of it.

My ship will not answer me. Of course there are several completely logical explanations for this, involving complications to the mission or an accident in space. But all of those possibilities presuppose the reality of my mission. To put it in plain English—the simplest explanation for why the spaceship won't answer my wibble is that it doesn't exist. It never existed. It's all in my mind.

I spent the past few hours scouring the Internet for information about empowerment fantasies and the ability of the human mind to protect itself by creative invention. There are many remarkable accounts of people who have constructed fantasy identities to lessen the pain of their real lives. Some of them even developed multiple personalities. I have tried to review this information with the dispassionate and critical eye of a Level-Five GC Evaluator. The more I have read, the more fearful I have become. I must admit that my circumstances fit the model perfectly.

It seemed very bad luck that aliens seeking a random human experience happened to select a boy from such an atypically unhappy home.

It is far more likely that a boy from such a background, pushed to desperation by bullying and abuse, should have sought refuge in a fantasy that allowed him to think he would have life or death powers over his tormentors.

I remember Ketchvar's first moments on Planet Earth. Tom Filber's mother was attacking with a broom. An alien would have to be extremely unfortunate to get beamed down to Earth and stumble right away into such a situation. On the other hand, parental abuse is a well-known trigger for young humans to retreat into fantasies.

And what were the odds that an alien would have sailed over the many towns and cities of New Jersey in a spaceship and randomly selected a fourteen-year-old boy who had been taunted as an alien by his peers?

I tremble to admit it, but it makes far more sense that such a beleaguered young Earthling would have taken the taunts hurled against him and used them to construct, in his mind, a kind of suit of armor: "I am not like you. You cannot really harm me. You call me 'alien,' so I will become a powerful alien. I will evaluate you and pass judgment upon you and then go back to my safe world."

It is two in the morning in a small room in a decrepit old house on Beech Avenue, and I cannot prove this or discount it. Every argument cuts both ways.

And what of Tom Filber? Is his consciousness and will really locked up in a Ragwellian Bubble? Or am I, Ketchvar III, really part of Tom Filber, a defense mechanism of his that has taken control for a while?

Of course, there is one way I could settle this. I could reverse the Thromborg Technique, separate from his brain, and slither back out his nose. That would prove I am a Sandovinian. But since there is no spaceship to beam me up, I would then be trapped on Earth, without even a shell, a slow-moving and defenseless gastropod.

So, at least for the time being, I am stuck here, trapped in the terrible limbo of not knowing the truth about my own identity. Or, to put it another way, I'm nearly positive that I am Ketchvar, but I can't prove it. And I also can't stop my mind from returning to the alternative, which is so frightening it literally knocks me off my feet.

I stand up from the desk and wrap my hands around my body. My knees feel weak and nausea hits. I double over and make retching sounds, but I have nothing to throw up.

I end up on the floor, curled in a fetal position.

What if I am really Tom Filber? What if I am a member of this foolish species—the laughingstock of the universe? Not only that, but I would then be the laughingstock of the laughingstock. Humans are a pathetic race, but a human who has to pretend he's an alien is the lowest of the low.

Suppose there is no spaceship to rescue me, and no Galactic Confederation to impose order on chaos. In other words, suppose this is my only real life and I'm stuck with it! I'm stuck with my mother and father, I'm stuck with my horrible sister, and most of all, I'm stuck with myself!

I crawl to the desk and slowly climb back up to the chair. I tilt my chin toward the sugar doughnut and whisper, "Come in, Preceptor. This is Ketchvar. I really need help. I fear prolonged exposure to humans is making me lose my sanity."

There is no answer from the wibbler. But in the reflection of the window I see a fourteen-year-old boy pleading his case to a stale doughnut wrapped in tinfoil, and I have to admit he looks ridiculous.

30

This is how it feels to be an endangered species.

Little kids on their way to elementary school pop out from behind hedges and aim finger ray guns at me. "Hey, Alien. Got you!"

If I was a piping plover I might soar into the sky or fly out over the surf.

Since I cannot take wing, I hurry up the hill and dart into Winthrop P. Muller High School. As soon as I walk past the security guard I can feel that things have changed for the worse.

The entire student body has now had a chance to read and digest my messages to the Preceptors. I have become a school celebrity, but in a very bad way. I keep my head down and hurry through the hallways, trying to pretend I don't hear their taunts and jibes.

"Yo, Snaily," a big football player shouts as I pass. "You try to crawl in through my nostril and I'll hawk you right back out and flush you."

His friends laugh. I veer away and run into a crowd of older girls who block my path. "Here's what I don't get," their blond leader says. "Why cross the whole galaxy just to take over the body of such a loser?"

I try to dodge around them, but they dissolve into a mist of highlighted hair and polished nails and reform again right in front of me. If I were a northern bog turtle I could pull my head into my shell and wait for them to lose interest and disperse, but a boy has no such easy escape.

"It could be part of his plan," a tall girl speculates with a laugh. "Those braces could be a secret antenna."

"Let's see if we can get him to power up." They pull out cell phones with built-in cameras and start flashing away at me. "Turn on your braces, Alien!"

"Send a message."

"Try to fly."

I break through the center of their pack, but I manage to take only a few steps before strong arms grab me. It's Jason Harbishaw, who has also apparently read my private messages. He throws me up against a locker. "So you felt good about hitting me with that acorn, huh?"

"I regret throwing it at you," I tell him honestly. "I am an evaluator and I shouldn't have interfered. My sister is a mean girl and she deserves what she gets."

He whispers, "You're the one who climbed our fence and scared my mom the other night, right? Do you have any idea what happens to people who mess with my family?"

A friend of his hisses, "Teacher!"

"You'll get yours," he promises, and pushes me away.

I back up fast and slam into a heavyset female teacher carrying a coffee mug. She stumbles and goes down. I would like to help her and make sure she didn't scald herself, but instead I take advantage of the shrieks and general confusion to sprint away.

Somehow I manage to make it through the gauntlet of dangers, survive the first three periods, and stagger into the trailer for English class just a few minutes late. Mrs. Hilderlee stands at the front, enthusiastically waving a copy of *Hamlet* as if she is trying to swat a wasp with it. She turns and begins writing something about "thine own self" on the board. I dart in from the doorway while her back is turned and tiptoe to my desk.

Michelle Peabody does not even glance at me as I slip into the seat next to her. She is wearing a V-necked blue sweater and her blond hair is tied with a red ribbon and falls over one shoulder. She has never looked lovelier.

I am tempted to whisper a few apologetic words to her. I would like her to know that I did not sleep a wink all night, and that I am truly sorry for any trouble I have caused her. She has a right to be angry—I see now that I should not have written about our kiss, even to the Preceptors. It was a private matter, and not GC business.

Scott sees the direction of my glance. "Careful, Romeo," he hisses.

We have both momentarily forgotten Mrs. Hilderlee, who has walked quietly up the row of desks and now stands right behind us, smiling. "No, not Romeo," she says. "Wrong play. This is *Hamlet*, and today we're going to look at some advice that Polonius gives his son, Laertes, who is about to leave Denmark to study in England. Of course in those days, such an ocean voyage was perilous, so Polonius didn't know if he was ever going to see his son again. He tries to condense all his worldly knowledge into a few pithy lines."

Her words make me think of my own father on Sandoval, and his recent goodbye to me. He knew I was going off on a dangerous space mission to Earth and he was not in the best of health. Sandovinians are not given to fancy speeches like Polonius, so he did not dispense advice and we did not exchange any terms of endearment.

I wonder now what was left unsaid. When he told me I might have to come home soon and run the Ketchvar burrow, was he hinting at more than his own infirmity? Was he very gently chiding me for becoming too caught up in the Galactic Confederation? Was it his way of suggesting I pay more attention to my own family?

I also think of Graham Filber walking home from the bar with me, and how our steps rose and fell in unison. I recall that on my first night on Planet Earth, when I crawled through the attic balcony, he suggested that I blamed him for marrying my mother and creating an unhappy home. He admitted that we weren't close, and took responsibility for it. He was clearly a lonely, disappointed but good-hearted man who needed a friendlier and more forgiving son.

For a moment the two fathers merge in my mind. They were both smart and gentle, both hid their pain, and now both have sunk out of sight without a word of farewell.

Mrs. Hilderlee has walked to the blackboard at the front

of the room. "First Polonius tells Laertes not to dress too fancily, and not to borrow money," she explains. "Then he finishes up with the most famous fatherly advice in all of English literature." Her eyes catch mine. "Tom, please read the last three lines."

I start to read, but the speech unexpectedly takes on such great personal relevance that I have trouble finishing it: " 'This above all: to thine own self be true.' " My voice quivers. I notice that Michelle Peabody has turned her head and is staring at me. " 'And it must follow, as the night the day, Thou canst not then be false to any man.' "

"Very good," Mrs. Hilderlee says. "Can you tell us what those words mean?"

I answer softly, "The most important thing in life is knowing who you really are. If you can just figure that out, everything else will fall into place." I do not add that right now I am not sure if I am a fourteen-year-old Earthling or a gastropod from a nebula. If I'm a human, my heart is on the left side of my body. If I'm a gastropod, I have an open circulatory system with a single-auricle pump located near my head. How can I be true to myself when I'm not sure about such basic things as my own heart? And how can anyone—especially a nice girl in a blue sweater—ever trust me?

"Bravo," Mrs. Hilderlee says. "That's a fine way of putting it. Now, I want everyone to write down ten 'To thine own self be true' moments."

The class groans, and Scott mutters, "If Shakespeare was here, I'd kick him in the gonads."

31

Somehow I manage to slink from class to class and hallway to hallway.

After gym I forgo showering and change clothes right by the locker room door, ready to call out for help if I am bullied. The large gray trash can that I was stuffed into stands nearby, a grim and stinky reminder of how bad things can get if I lower my guard.

By the time biology rolls around, I am exhausted but liberation is in sight. I just have to make it through whatever Mr. Karnovsky has in store for us, coast through last period, and then I will be out the door. I have no intention of going to any after-school activities. There is no point in discussing ways to help endangered species when you are clinging to existence by your own splintering fingernails.

We walk in the door of the science classroom and take our seats. Mr. Karnovsky steps out of the supply room in his usual white lab jacket, but he does not begin a lesson.

He just stands there, looking at us. There is an unexpected sadness in his gray eyes.

"I'm sorry," he says, "but I don't think I can teach today. I've just found something out that . . . knocked me for a loop. He was a very special man and . . . I don't . . ."

He breaks off and focuses his eyes on some test tubes on a rack by the window. "When I first came to this school, twenty years ago, I was afraid of public speaking," he confesses. For a moment, everyone has forgotten that there is an alien in their midst. The class is watching Mr. Karnovsky, trying to figure out what is wrong with him. "The idea of standing up in front of a room of students filled me with terror," he admits. "Luckily, there was a wise and generous older science teacher here, who took me under his wing."

Mr. Karnovsky smiles at the memory. "He was very vigorous in those days. He and his wife had just come back from a trip to Australia, with pictures of the Great Barrier Reef. They had gone swimming with the sharks. When you meet someone who is that full of life, you think they will live forever."

I start to get a hunch where Mr. Karnovsky may be going with this. I sincerely hope I am wrong.

"As he got older and his health started to break down, he never lost his love for nature, and his concern for this planet," Mr. Karnovsky continues. "It was so like him that even in his last days, instead of thinking about himself, he founded a club at this school focused on the future and the need to save the world."

Mr. Karnovsky takes off his eyeglasses and polishes them on his lab coat. He blinks out at us and looks ten years younger. "I know he wasn't teaching much at the end, so I doubt that many of you had much contact with him. But Arthur Stringfellow was a wonderful presence at this school for four decades, and his death this morning has just . . . Well . . . I simply can't teach today. So I want to show you some videos he shot, and ask you in his memory to go out and plant a tree or throw out some trash or try to make the earth a little better place."

He wheels out a monitor and bends to plug it in.

"Home movies!" Scott whispers. "Get the popcorn."

"Don't get your hopes up. This is definitely going to be PG," Zitface grumbles.

We are soon watching old videos of a trek through a rain forest. The camera picks out birds and monkeys, and verdant trees and flowers. The viewpoint unexpectedly shifts as the camera is passed to someone else, and the lens is trained on a middle-aged Arthur Stringfellow paddling a kayak through a flooded rain forest. His wife sits behind him, and they look happier than any humans I have encountered.

I sit there watching them and remembering the weak but fearless old man who sucked oxygen and demanded that we all do our part to save the earth.

When I told him that I couldn't worry about the Hoosaguchee River because I needed to take care of myself, he replied that he had a few problems, too. Now I realize that he was dying, and he probably knew it, and I feel ashamed.

My feeling of shame builds steadily. I make it out of school alive and head home, keeping to the shadows and dodging my way toward Beech Avenue. When I'm halfway home, I hear kids' loud voices and dive into some roadside shrubs. I peek out from the leafy cover and watch a few of my schoolmates walk past. They're laughing and having fun, and they couldn't have cared less whether I was there or not. I untangle my left leg from a vine and pull a few thorns out of my wrist. For a moment I imagine Mr. Stringfellow looking down at me, frowning, as if to ask: "How can you live this way?"

I hurry up to my room and shut my door. There is still no word from the spaceship. I sit for several hours, playing Galactic Warrior and hiding out in my locked bedroom. Finally I switch off the computer.

No, this is not going to work. I may be marooned on Earth indefinitely. It's even possible that Miss Schroeder is right and this is—and always has been—my permanent home. I've wasted a beautiful fall day cowering in fear.

Mr. Stringfellow said the mark of a man is how he deals with adversity. It's no use slinking from hiding place to hiding place and hoping that I'll be rescued. If I'm stuck on Planet Earth, for a day or a lifetime, then I might as well step up to the plate and try to act like a man. And suddenly I know just what to do to honor Mr. Stringfellow's memory.

I get some gear together: dark jeans, a black shirt, a camera, a flashlight, and a length of rope. As the sun sets, I dress in my ninja outfit, stow the stuff in a small bag, and head downstairs.

32

My mother is on the phone in the kitchen, calling various friends of my dad to see if any of them have heard from him. From the drained look on her face, I can tell that there is no news.

I slip by her, out the back door, and head for the garage to get my bicycle. A creaking sound makes me stop. Michelle's swing is moving back and forth in the evening breeze.

For a moment I hesitate. I'm pretty sure she wants nothing more to do with me. But I have decided to be brave tonight, and this seems like the logical place to start.

I find the path through the hedge and walk over to her. "Greetings, Michelle," I call out. "Do not be alarmed. It is not a stranger, come to harm you. It is only me, Tom Filber."

"You already hurt me," she says.

"I know. I'm sorry. I should not have written to the Preceptors about you. It was not a Galactic Confederation matter. What happened between us should have stayed between us."

She glances at me and then quickly away. "Nothing happened between us."

"Yes, you are right," I agree, and lower my voice. "But I would still like to apologize for going for tongue action. As crazy as I know this sounds, it was not my idea. Tom Filber has had a crush on you for many years. In a moment of weakness, I listened to his foolish advice."

How dare you tell her that? Tom's furious voice demands from the Ragwellian Bubble.

Because it's true, I respond. *You did have a crush on her.*

I can feel him hurling his consciousness against the sides of the bubble in a rage. *You have no right to talk to her about me! This is a low-down betrayal. I'll get you back for this!*

I'm just trying to be honest, I tell him. *Now shut up.*

"Who are you telling to shut up?" Michelle asks. Apparently I have mumbled a few words out loud.

"I was talking to myself," I tell her quickly. "I was telling myself to 'step up' and take the blame for my own actions. I may be stuck on Earth for a while, so I have decided to live by a human code of conduct and try to act like an honorable man."

She peers up at me. "You really believe that stuff, don't you?"

"What stuff?"

"The letters you wrote, about being from a sand planet."

"It's called Sandoval, but there's not much sand. It's swampy. And very beautiful."

She studies my face in the moonlight. "This isn't just a joke? In your mind you really think it's true?"

"I hope it's true," I tell her. "Sometimes I don't know myself. My spaceship is not answering my calls. I'm confused and scared right now."

She seems to like me when I'm honest and vulnerable. "Climb up on the swing for a minute. Sit over there. Don't try to touch me or I'll scream."

I climb up on the swing and sit across from her. Our feet push the swing back and forth.

"You sounded a little scared today, when you read that speech in class," she says.

I nod, and recite the line: " 'This above all: to thine own self be true.' " For an intense moment Michelle and I look right into each other's eyes. "I was realizing that it's pretty hard to be true to my own self, if I don't know who I am," I tell her. "Maybe that's one reason I didn't treat you the way you deserved to be treated. I'm very sorry."

"It does feel like you've changed a lot in the last week," she replies softly. "I've lived next to you all my life, and I sense that you're very different. But it's more likely that you're just crazy than that you're really an alien." She smiles. "No offense."

I smile back. "None taken. Miss Schroeder agrees with you. She thinks it's just an empowerment fantasy. I'm a little worried that she could be right, and I might really be

Tom Filber, stuck here forever on Planet Earth, and driven over the edge by bullying and my lousy home life. But deep down, I know where I'm from, Michelle."

"You've never said my name like that before," she whispers.

"Like what?"

She doesn't answer. Her blue eyes glint.

I get up and slide over to her side of the swing and sit down next to her. "Like what?" I repeat.

"Where are you from, Tom?"

I raise a finger heavenward. "There's the constellation humans call Orion, the Hunter. You see those three bright stars in a row? Those make up his belt—Alnitak, Alnilam, and Mintaka. To the right of Mintaka, can you see a very faint gleam? Sandoval's sun is midway in that nebula."

She has followed my finger and is staring up at the stars. "You do seem to know an awful lot about astronomy," she breathes. She slowly lowers her gaze to look back at me and it must be an illusion, but for a moment the red suns of Sandoval seem to be gilding her face. Her blue eyes flame dark purple and her cheeks are flushed.

I am tempted to kiss her again. But I do not. When I got on the swing she warned me not to touch her. I stand up very fast and try to control myself. "I should go now."

"Where?" she asks.

"The river."

"At this time of night?"

"I am tired of hiding in my room, waiting for the world

to leave me alone," I tell her. "Clearly that is never going to happen. I want to take an action. I am going on a quest to honor Mr. Stringfellow's memory. I promised him I would do it, and I will."

She stands up. "No, *we* promised him we would do it."

"Isn't it late for you?" I ask.

"The Goth concert will probably last another hour, and the drummer looks a little drunk." She hesitates. "I really want to come. But what exactly are we going to do?"

"I think the paint factory may be dumping chemical waste into the river," I tell her. "I want to get proof."

"That sounds dangerous."

"My plan is to slip in quietly, now that everyone is gone, get the proof, and slip out." I would love her to come on this trip with me, but I have pledged to be honorable and responsible. I remember the guard who woke me from my Flindarian Lapse on the bank of the Hoosaguchee. He claimed dogs patrolled the property. I do not believe this. There were also supposed to be dogs at the Harbishaw mansion, but it was just a bluff. I never heard so much as a bark. "The truth is I can't promise it will be completely safe. And I don't want to get you into trouble or put you in danger."

"You won't be getting me into trouble," Michelle says. "I'm making this decision for myself. Mr. Stringfellow was a cool guy. And I don't like sitting out here on a swing any more than you like hiding in your room. Anyway, I'm already dressed perfectly for the occasion." I see that she's wearing black jeans and a dark top. "Do you want my company or not?" she asks.

I climb off the swing and offer her my hand, and she takes it. Her fingers feel warm in mine. She hops off after me, and we head away together.

33

The streetlights stop where the houses do, and we ride on, side by side, in the moonlight. It is a cool fall night, but the excitement of a shared adventure keeps me warm. We are really going to do this! I have a strange sense that this is what it means to be young and human—to take a risk and try to accomplish something, even if there are very real dangers crowding in from the shadows.

The river soon gleams ahead of us, a glittering black band that catches starlight like cosmic flypaper. Its musky throat-clogging stench grows stronger, and when we turn onto River Road I can hear it trying to crawl up the bank in an endless scurrying of tiny wavelets.

"Where to now?" Michelle asks.

"This way," I tell her, and we head northward. Factories loom on both sides of the river. In the moonlight I can just make out the K of Kinderly Plastics Works.

We reach the end of River Road and I show her the spot

beneath a tree where we can conceal our bikes. "You've been here before?" she whispers.

"Once," I tell her. "We just follow the river." I lead her along the muddy bank. Our sneakers make little sucking sounds as they rise and fall.

"It sure is dark," she whispers.

"Darkness is our friend," I tell her. "As long as we're in our ninja outfits."

Now that we are taking a decisive action, my mind is clearer and sharper than it has been for two days. I could probably muster the concentration needed for a Flindarian Lapse, but I can't ask Michelle to wait on the mud bank while I search the stars. There is, however, something I can do to show her why this night mission is so important.

"Take this camera for a second," I tell her. "It's time to film some wildlife."

She looks around. "There's nothing here."

"Not yet." I point to the river. "Keep watching."

She peers out. "What's out there? The Loch Ness Monster?"

"Something even better," I tell her. I clear my mind, but instead of throwing my essence skyward in a Flindarian Lapse, I use the Schusterfong Summons to call upon a fellow living creature. Since I've seen this river dweller before, I know exactly how to try to reach out to it.

To accomplish the Schusterfong Summons, I plug my ears with my index fingers and open my mouth as wide as possible. My tongue lolls out, and I begin to softly ululate. I realize I must look ridiculous.

The camera dangles down from Michelle's wrist as she stares at me. She asks very nervously: "Tom, what's going on? Are you having a fit?"

It's difficult to answer her while I am Schusterfonging. "The camera," I ululate.

"What about it?"

"Raise. Aim. There!"

A tiny sparkle of reflected moonlight threads its way through the shallows. "What is it?" she asks.

"A brown speckled mucker," I ululate. "Get a shot."

She raises the camera and starts filming. The mucker swims to the surface and does a half roll. The moonlight reflects off the sequinlike scales on its belly. It's very close now. Michelle hits the flash, and for a moment I can see its entire three-inch shape, from its tapered mouth to the brown speckles that begin near its gill cover and run down to its bluish caudal tail fin. Then, as if deciding that we've all had enough fun, it disappears into the deeper water, and I snap out of the Schusterfong.

"Did you get it?" I ask her.

"See for yourself." She plays it back for me on the camera's small screen. The fish can be seen clearly, turning on its back and reflecting light back at us with its belly scales. "What's the big deal about it?"

"The brown speckled mucker is highly endangered," I explain. "It's on state and federal lists. If the Harbishaws are dumping stuff into the river near an endangered species, they're in really big trouble."

She nods, and we turn to look at the giant paint factory.

Its twin smokestacks tower above us like black pillars holding up the dark clouds of the night sky. "How are we going to get in?" she whispers.

"Hop the fence. I brought pliers to bend down the wires at the top. Ready?"

"One question first," she says. "If that fish is so rare and endangered, how did you know it was going to be here?"

"This is where it lives," I tell her. "I saw one swimming in this bend of the river the last time I came."

"But how did you know it would swim up to the bank? You started making that strange sound and then it came right to us."

I smile at her. "That was one of my special alien powers. Or it could just have been good timing and dumb luck. Take your pick." I'm trying to turn this into a joke, but Michelle is studying my face and she's not laughing. "What's wrong?" I ask.

"I'm starting to like you," she confesses, "and I'm not sure whether I'd rather have you turn out to be a crazy boy or a perfectly sane snail creature."

"Either way, I like you, too," I whisper back. "And I'm real glad you came. It wouldn't be much fun to do this alone."

She nods. "Yeah, it's dark and creepy. Let's go before I lose my nerve."

34

The wire fence that surrounds the Harbishaw paint factory is fifteen feet high. We follow its curving perimeter, passing signs that warn: PRIVATE PROPERTY. NO TRESPASSING. KEEP OUT.

"I don't think we're going to find a hole," Michelle says.

"We don't need one," I tell her. "We're going to go over it, not through it. But we do need a little privacy."

We soon come to a cluster of trees that screen a section of fence from the factory. I take the pliers out of the bag, clench them between my teeth, and start climbing. The chinks in the fence are the perfect size for handholds and footholds, and I reach the top in seconds.

Needle-sharp spikes poke up every few inches. I grab the pliers and start bending the spikes down till I've flattened out a two-foot section. "Come on up," I whisper.

Michelle climbs as I swing myself over the top and head down. A tree has fallen over inside, so that its broken trunk leans against the fence and makes a nice landing pad. From the tree trunk I hop to the ground, and in a few seconds Michelle joins me there. "I can't believe we're really doing this," she marvels softly.

"Let's go finish the job," I whisper back, and lead her toward the dark factory.

We cross the deserted parking lot. As we approach the back of the building, I spot a loading dock. The door suddenly opens, and a man appears holding a flashlight. I pull Michelle behind one of the few cars left in the lot.

I steal a peek around the side of the fender and spot a security guard in a brown uniform. The beam from his flashlight darts around the parking lot and for a long moment shines right on our hiding place. "He's seen us," Michelle gasps.

"I don't think so," I respond. "He's just looking around."

His footsteps approach our car from the far side. "He's coming," she whispers. "Let's run for it."

"We'd never make it. Better to hide," I tell her and squirm under the car. She follows my example, and we're soon lying side by side beneath the chassis, watching the security guard's boots approach.

He stops so near to us that I can hear his breathing. If he shines his flashlight under the car he'll find us for sure. I take Michelle's hand in the darkness and give her a reassuring squeeze. She squeezes back. We're both holding our breath.

The guard circles the car and then slowly walks off. We

listen to his footsteps recede until they fade into the silence of the night.

"He might come back," Michelle whispers.

"No, he's gone," I tell her, rolling out from under the car. "But that was a close call. Why don't you head back out and wait for me outside the fence?"

She gets to her feet next to me. "Who said anything about heading back? We just need to be careful."

We hurry toward the building, and I feel a surge of self-doubt. What is a Level-Five GC Evaluator doing breaking into a guarded factory? Come to think of it, it's probably not smart behavior for a fourteen-year-old boy, either. But we've come too far to turn back. For Mr. Stringfellow and also for myself, on some deep level I know I have to see this through. Michelle doesn't seem inclined to turn back, either. So on we go, step by step toward the back of the enormous building.

We reach the loading dock and see a parked tanker truck. Red letters on its side warn: CENTRAL JERSEY FILTRATION PLANT. DANGER—HAZARDOUS MATERIALS. The side of the truck is labeled with HAZMAT and EPA insignias. Could I be wrong? Does this factory send its chemical waste to a treatment plant and pay for it to be filtered?

I remember the chemical stench I smelled the first night I came to the river, and how badly the security guard wanted to get me out of there. And I recall how the river itself seemed to cry out to me. All my instincts tell me we're on the right track and should keep going.

A thick black hose runs from a pump on the tanker

truck through the loading dock door. "I'm gonna see where that hose leads," I tell Michelle. "If anybody comes, give a whistle. Try to make it sound like a birdcall."

I dart out of hiding, and Michelle stays right with me. "I'm not great on birdcalls," she explains, and pushes in the door ahead of me. The door swings shut behind us, and we enter the bowels of the giant factory.

The low-ceilinged corridors are lit by fluorescent lights set far apart. We follow the hose around dark twists and turns to a basement level that opens into a storage chamber. Warnings are posted: DANGER—TOXINS.

"There!" I whisper. Several dozen giant containers sit shoulder to shoulder on wooden pallets, arranged in rows. Each container is more than ten feet high and must weigh several hundred pounds. They are labeled DANGER—HAZARDOUS WASTE.

I raise the camera to film them, but Michelle touches my arm and whispers: "I hear something."

Men's voices ring out. We duck into a corner of the storage chamber, behind some wooden crates. The voices get louder—they're heading our way. I poke the camera lens through a hole in a crate and peer at the viewfinder.

Two men appear, one tall and the other broad-shouldered and squat. They take the black hose that runs down from the truck and attach it to a container in the front row. I can hear the liquid being sucked out by the pump. The waste is going into the tanker truck. The two men repeat this procedure a dozen times. Soon, all the containers in the front row are empty.

But they don't start draining the second row or the third. Instead one of the men says, "That's plenty for the truck. Has Al seen the old man?"

"Yeah, he went up to the office to get his cut. He'll play with the numbers for us, no problem."

"Fine. Then let's flush the rest."

They have a second hose ready. It's bright red and doesn't come from the truck, but rather is attached to a web of piping that runs across the ceiling. They use this red hose to drain container after container. I close my eyes and can almost feel the chemical waste being sucked out of the containers, into the piping of the factory, and then discharged beneath the surface of the Hoosaguchee.

"You ever swim in this river?" the tall man asks.

"You kidding?" his friend replies. "Might as well swim in a toilet."

"I meant when you were a kid."

"Yeah, sure. But that was twenty years ago. Now I got a pool."

"You've got a pool? You son of a bitch. When are you going to invite me over?"

"That would be never."

I record everything they say and do. They work methodically, and they've soon drained the second row of containers and have started on the third. Michelle and I try to keep still and silent, but we're kneeling in a very narrow hiding place and my arms and legs start to cramp. I stretch out a little and lean back against the side of a wooden crate. It buckles with a cracking sound.

"What was that?" the tall man asks.

"Didn't hear nothing," his friend replies.

I do my best to brace the cracked wooden crate, but it cracks again and a large shard breaks off and crashes to the floor.

"Mice?" the squat man asks.

"More likely we've got a rat," the tall man surmises, and I hear a nasty hardness in his voice.

I peer out through the crack and see that he's pulled out a club and is heading our way.

I kneel next to Michelle and whisper, "This time we can't hide. They'll find us for sure. We've got to run for it."

"Where?" she asks.

"I don't know. Deeper into the factory, till we can find an exit."

She looks scared, but I can't blame her. My own knees are knocking together. "Okay," she whispers. "Say when."

I count, "One, two, three," and then we're off, sprinting through the back of the storage chamber into a dark hallway.

I hear the tall man cry out, "THERE THEY GO. CALL SECURITY!"

35

We race through the darkness. Footsteps ring out behind us and men call to each other. I haven't been this scared since my spaceship was caught in a meteor shower on the way to Omicron XII.

Michelle trips and almost falls. "I can't see anything," she says. "Where's the flashlight?"

"If I turn it on, they'll spot us right away," I tell her. "Take my hand."

She fumbles in the darkness, and then I feel her warm palm in my own.

I blink my eyes five times in rapid succession and convert Tom Filber's ocular processes to a Penteluvian Vision Stream. The Penteluvians live their entire lives in extremely low light and have developed a method of sight-sensing their way through almost pitch darkness.

Of course, it's also possible that I'm really Tom Filber, and I'm so scared I'm blundering through the gloom on adrenaline and dumb luck.

A new and terrifying sound reaches us. At first it's faint and I think it's the night wind whooshing through an open window. But it comes again, louder and closer and repeating itself in bloodcurdling variations.

It sounds like a platoon of ghosts calling out to us. There's a hunger in the sound, a message of sharp danger. Whoever is bellowing into the night is following us, tracking us. And then the sound echoes more clearly, and I recognize it and feel a sharp stab of terror.

It's the baying of dogs. The factory does have them after all, and they're being used to hunt us!

"Tom!"

"I'm sorry I brought you into this."

"No, I wanted to come. But I'm really scared."

"Me, too," I admit. "But if we don't panic, maybe we can find a way out. Once we get over the fence, the dogs can't chase us. Let's try this way."

We push through a doorway marked with warning signs and I shut the heavy door and lock it behind us. That should slow the pursuit for a while.

We must have entered the wing of the factory where chemical processes take place. I see the shadowy outlines of chemical drums. The stench is acrid. It burns my nose and scalds my throat. "I can't breathe," Michelle gasps.

"Pull your shirt over your mouth," I tell her, and lead her on quickly.

"I feel light-headed," she whispers. "I think I'm going to faint."

"We're almost out," I encourage her. But I am also feeling

dizzy. If we don't get out in a few seconds, these fumes will knock us both unconscious. My legs are unsteady, and I'm already half supporting Michelle.

"Tom, I'm not going to make it."

I look around desperately and spot a red EMERGENCY EXIT light. "There's a door," I tell her.

Her legs give out, and I catch her and carry her to the emergency exit. I kick the door open. An alarm shrills. But the good news is that we're back outside. I gulp in cold breaths of fresh night air.

The bad news is that we've emerged at the bottom of a steep flight of stone steps. I'm still groggy from the fumes, and I don't know if I could stagger up those stairs on my own. Michelle is semiconscious. There's no way she'll be able to climb them.

On the other hand, we don't have a choice. The dogs are racing through the factory at high speed, and they've clearly picked up our scent. Their baying gets closer and closer.

"We've got to climb these steps," I tell Michelle. "Breathe in fresh air. I can't do this without your help."

She makes a sound in her throat. Her arm hangs limp.

I drape her over my shoulder and bend low to center her weight. Then I lift and stagger up the first step. Somehow I make it up the second one.

My strength gives out, I totter for a second, and then I collapse and fall. Michelle lands heavily on top of me.

The dogs sound excited. Maybe they can sense that we're trapped. They'll burst through the emergency door in seconds, their sharp teeth flashing in the moonlight.

I have run out of options. What a sad way for a highly trained GC evaluator to meet his end. I think of my poor father, lost in the ooze of Sandoval. Anything seems preferable to being torn apart by dogs.

I fish around in the darkness in my pocket. Find the tinfoil with the stale sugar doughnut. Whisper into my wibbler, "Come in, please. This is Ketchvar. I'm in terrible danger. I NEED HELP RIGHT NOW!"

There is no response. I draw back my arm in fury. I am ready to fling the useless sugar doughnut into the darkness when I suddenly hear the crackle of interstellar space static. A second later the Preceptor's distinctive voice asks faintly, "Ketchvar?"

"Yes, Preceptor! I can barely hear you."

The Preceptor's words are mostly lost in the vastness of space. I only catch bits and pieces. "Emergency rescue mission . . . Bubos VII . . . microtic plague . . . Still in transit . . ."

"I NEED HELP RIGHT NOW," I shout into the wibbler. "I'm about to be torn apart by dogs!" Michelle groans softly, as if to remind me of her presence. "I'm with a human female. The two of us require immediate assistance. It's a matter of life and death."

"Try our best . . ." the voice promises. ". . . Limit to what we can do from here."

36

feel a tingling sensation. It's a reverse gravity beam reaching out to us from hundreds of light-years in space. It can't lift us up the steps from such a distance, but it's making Michelle feel a bit lighter.

I get to my knees and then to my feet. Drape her over my shoulder again. And I start climbing.

The night sky is visible high above us and I stagger toward it, moving very slowly, step by step, from an abyss of darkness and fear toward the familiar safety of the glittering stars.

Now you know for certain who you are! I encourage myself. Your GC colleagues are coming back to rescue you and take you home. They're all in the ship, gathered on the main deck, watching you on their deep space screen. The Preceptor Supervisor is no doubt pacing from one of his five legs to the other in that nervous way of his. His scaly orange-yellow face is tight with worry as he tries to make sure they're doing everything they can to help you! Don't let them down! Do it for Sandoval!

I've carried Michelle more than halfway up the steps, but I'm running out of steam. So I shift gears and motivation.

You're a young man for the time being—you've assumed the body of an Earthling, I remind myself. If you don't make it up these steps, no one will ever know about the chemical waste being pumped into the river. So act like a man! Mr. Stringfellow was right. You have no right to stand on the sidelines. You may be a Sandovinian, but this is your most noble human moment! Go for it!

So I go for it. I'm three-quarters of the way up now. I can see the top step. Even with the reverse gravity beam helping, my arms are aching and my legs feel like strands of limp spaghetti. Tom Filber's panicked voice seeps out from the Ragwellian Bubble. *You'll never make it. You idiot snail creature. You've taken over my body only to lead us both to ruin. We'll be ripped apart by the dogs . . .*

I reseal the bubble and put all thoughts of pain and failure out of my mind. I can do this. I must find a way! I keep climbing. And as I stagger up the final few steps, I have an insight that this is exactly what it means to be human. To blunder along, bravely putting one foot in front of the other. The whole species is climbing step by step out of darkness, bearing a heavy weight. They are aware of their predicament. They have no idea what is waiting for them at the top of the stairs. But they are fighting their way up toward the stars as best they can.

I near the top step. Michelle gasps, "Tom?"

"Breathe the night air," I encourage her.

Two more steps to go. One more. I reach the top and feel triumphant for one long second. Then I see the barrier in front of me.

It's some sort of concrete retaining wall that circles this part of the factory. It looks about six feet high. And there's no way around it.

The dogs have stopped baying and started growling. I can hear their paws scrabbling at the closed emergency door. The guards will come and open it for them, and they'll bound up the steep steps and attack us!

No, I won't let it end this way. It occurs to me that this wall, which now seems an insurmountable obstacle, will guarantee our safety from the dogs if I can get us over it.

"I've hit a wall, literally," I shout into the wibbler. "Give the beam the full juice. Redirect the Furnasian Thrusters. I need all the help you can give me!"

"Tom, who are you talking to?" Michelle whispers. She's still groggy, but she sounds a bit stronger.

The beam intensifies. The tingling sensation is more pronounced. I step to the wall. There are no handholds or footholds. "Hold me tight," I tell Michelle. "Don't let me go."

"I'll never let you go," she promises. I feel her arms gripping me a little more tightly. I step onto a rock and reach up.

Voices ring out from inside the factory. Men call to each

other: "They must have gone through that door! Good, then they're trapped! Let the dogs at them."

I stretch and my fingers find the top of the wall. I get the best grip I can, kick upward, and pull with all my strength. A surge of adrenaline helps. And of course the reverse gravity beam is making us both much lighter. But even so, I'm not going to make it. Who am I kidding? There's no way I can carry the two of us over this wall. My arms aren't strong enough. My fingers are slipping.

I hear a thud from down below. The emergency door is kicked open. Paws bound up stone steps. I can hear the dogs jockeying for position, straining to be first to get at us. The furious growls promise us pain.

I search deep inside myself and find the strength for one last effort. This has very little to do with the reverse gravity beam. This is pure Ketchvar, and maybe a little of Tom Filber tossed in. The first dog leaps and his teeth graze the bottom of my foot, but I pull with everything I have and lift us to the top of the wall.

I glance back down for one second. Five dogs snarl and leap furiously. I see three guards climbing the steep stone steps. One of them raises a flashlight and shines it at us. "There!" he calls. "How could they possibly climb that?"

I don't stick around to answer his question. I transfer my weight, hang down the other side of the wall, and drop to the ground. "Michelle, we're safe now, but we have to hurry to the fence," I tell her. "Can you walk?"

"I think so," she says, and takes a few tentative steps.

37

We hurry to the fence. I could wibble the spaceship and ask for the reverse gravity beam again, but there's no need. Michelle seems to be recovering quickly.

She steps onto the split tree trunk, grasps the fence, and starts pulling herself up. I climb right next to her, encouraging her. We reach the top and swing our legs over the bent spikes at nearly the same moment.

We pause there for a moment, as a familiar but still-frightening canine howl pierces the cold night air. The guards must have taken the dogs back through the factory and let them out a different exit. It sounds like they picked up our scent outside the concrete wall and are now racing toward us at full speed.

Michelle shivers when she hears the dogs, but she also looks proud. "We finished the job," she whispers.

"We've got the goods," I agree. "Now let's get out of here." We climb down and leap to the ground.

Michelle can now manage a jerky half run—she'll soon

be one hundred percent recovered. We pick our way as fast as we can along the muddy bank toward the spot where we hid our bikes.

I throw a glance at the dark band of river. Even in its polluted condition, it's home to a variety of wildlife. The animals and fish should have an easier, cleaner time of it in the months ahead.

Just as we reach our bikes, I hear angry growling in the distance and a furious metallic rattle. The dogs must have made it to the wire fence and are leaping against it, furious that we've gotten away again. Seconds later the guards' frustrated voices ring out. One of them shouts, "Somebody get a car. They can't be far."

We push off on our bikes and race up River Road, two dark shadows speeding along with only the whirring of our pedals and the spinning of our wheels against the pavement to break the silence. I glance over at Michelle, bent low over her handlebars, and it occurs to me that I've had more excitement and taken more risks in this one night on Earth than in the last thousand years as a GC evaluator.

We turn onto the first side street and then veer down a narrow lane. The lots are small here, and the houses are dark and silent. We stop and watch through the narrow gap between two houses as a jeep races up River Road from the direction of the factory. Its high beams are on, and it must be going one hundred miles per hour as it roars past us and speeds away into the night.

Michelle looks back at me and raises her right hand. I believe she is signaling that she wants to indulge in a common human celebratory gesture known as a "high five." I slap her palm with my own, and suddenly I am flooded with a feeling of shared triumph and exultation, and we both smile.

We hurry home, stow the bikes in our garages, and meet by her swing. "That was a pretty awesome adventure," she says, looking excited and victorious.

"Swing?" I suggest. "To celebrate that we made it back in one piece."

She checks her watch. "Only for a minute. It's pretty late."

I climb on the swing first and she slides over next to me.

"Are you sure you're okay?" I ask. "You were pretty woozy back there."

"I'm fine now," she assures me. "I just needed some fresh air. Those chemicals reeked."

"Same ones they're dumping into the river," I point out. "Or were dumping. Because I think we can put a stop to it now." I hold up the camera.

"What are you going to do with the pictures?" she asks.

"We should probably turn them over to the *Barrisford Gazette*. Or to a local TV station."

Michelle thinks that over and looks just a little worried. "You do it, Tom. The trip was your idea."

"You shared the risks. You should share the credit."

"We did a good thing tonight," she says with pride. "But we were trespassing. My father wouldn't be happy about that. I think I'd better keep my name out of it."

"Okay," I agree. "I guess the important thing is that *we* both know we did it together. You're not sorry you came along?"

"Do you even have to ask that?" She gives my arm a squeeze. "It was the most exciting thing I've ever done."

"Me, too."

"Really?" She flashes me a grin. "I thought you crossed space at the speed of light and visited strange worlds."

"True," I tell her, "but I've never hidden under a car or been attacked by dogs before." She's still grinning, and I smile back. "You don't believe a word I say, do you?"

"I don't know what to believe about you," Michelle admits. "You're full of surprises. I keep thinking of you climbing that fence with the pliers in your teeth. You looked like a pirate."

"I was scared."

"You didn't show it." She checks her watch. "It's late. I should go." But she doesn't make a move to leave.

Go for it, Tom Filber encourages from the Ragwellian Bubble. *Can't you see the way she's looking at you? Tell her that her eyes are sparkling.*

Shut up, I order him. *This is your very last warning.*

But it's true. Her eyes are indeed glowing. "You have the prettiest eyes," I hear myself say.

She replies by just whispering my name. "Tom."

"No," I whisper back. "Ketchvar."

"That's a silly name. I prefer Tom."

"Whatever."

I do not want to destroy the camaraderie and good feeling we've built up on this night by misreading the signals and trying to kiss her. But my lips are being drawn to hers by a force stronger than our spaceship's suction beam. It takes all my GC training to resist it.

She looks up at me and asks softly, "Tom, what happened at the factory? I remember fainting, and you carried me through some kind of door. Then there were steps, and a wall. The dogs were closing in on us. How did we escape?"

"I wibbled my spaceship . . ."

"I remember you pleading for help. But there was no answer."

"They were in deep space," I tell her. "But they turned on their antigravity beam."

Our faces are now so close that I can feel her breath on my lips. "I don't recall a magic beam," she says. "I remember you carrying me on your back up the steps."

"How could I possibly climb a flight of steep steps with you on my back?"

"And then I remember you somehow getting us over that wall," she continues. "You told me to hold on tight, and I did. I trusted you. And you came through. I don't remember any spaceship. I just remember you."

The next thing I know, we're kissing. This time Michelle doesn't seem surprised or freaked out. I think she might even be the one who made the first move.

The night wind blows our swing slowly back and forth. Crickets chirp in the tall grass. Michelle's lips feel soft and taste sweet.

Go for tongue action, comes the advice from the Ragwellian Bubble. *This time I guarantee you're golden.*

I warned you that was your last chance. I will the Ragwellian Bubble out of Tom Filber's parietal lobe. It passes quickly through the blood-brain barrier into his circulatory system, is washed through the celiac artery into the stomach, and from there slips into the colon.

Get me out of this stinking cave, his voice pleads. *I was just trying to help.*

But I don't need his help, and I couldn't care less about tongue action. I'm enjoying being this close to Michelle. And even while I lose myself in the moment, part of me is remembering Romeo and Juliet, and the way Shakespeare based the end of his greatest love story on the power of a kiss. I may have to re-evaluate my opinions about Earth's great artists. I recognize now that Shakespeare may actually have understated things!

Michelle finally breaks away. Her cheeks are red, and she is breathing in excited little gulps. "I'd better go in," she says. "Even the Goths must have quit by now."

"Probably," I whisper. "Good night. Sleep tight."

"Don't let the bedbugs bite," she whispers back, and she kisses me one last time. "Oh, I forgot, you *are* a bedbug."

"Snail," I tell her. "Not even close."

38

Michelle goes into her house, and I hear the door swing shut behind her. I stay out on the swing, alone, looking up at the stars.

It's been a wild night of adventure and romance, and I admit I have felt more human than Sandovinian. But I know what I have to do next.

I take out my wibbler, and whisper, "Come in. Ketchvar here."

The Preceptor Supervisor's voice answers immediately. "Ketchvar! We've been so worried about you. We were in deep space, beyond communication range. We've read all your messages. What a time you've had! Are you okay?"

"Yes. It has been difficult. But I've managed to survive and I learned a great deal about humans."

"It sounds like they've treated you terribly. The species should be terminated. Shall we extract you right away? We have the reverse gravity beam ready."

I look over to the empty part of the bench where

Michelle was seated barely five minutes ago. "No, let's not do anything rash. Things are under control now. And I need a little more time to complete my evaluation and wrap up a few loose ends."

"Are you sure? Some of your messages sounded pretty desperate."

"Yes, I'm sure," I tell him. I hesitate for a second. "Is there any news about my father?"

"A search party located him in a deep mud hole. The temperature had dropped low, and he was nearly frozen."

I sit there on the swing, staring up at the stars, and it feels as if the cold night wind of Planet Earth is blowing right through my body. I ask in a low voice, "Could they save him?"

"The best doctors on Sandoval are taking care of him. He's resting comfortably now. We relayed your concern to him through GC channels. Your father sent a message back that you should finish your mission. But after you finish it, he said, you should come home."

For a moment it feels like I am floating off the swing, dizzy and delirious, somersaulting high into space. "Tell him I got his message and I will be home very soon," I say. "I'd better go in the house now. Even in the crazy Filber household, if I stay out too late somebody may eventually notice."

39

The two articles appear on the front page of the *Barrisford Gazette*. The first is the lead story of the day. A banner headline in the upper right-hand corner screams: PAINT COMPANY CAUGHT DUMPING WASTE INTO HOOSA-GUCHEE. A subheadline in smaller print proclaims: "Student Film Exposes Environmental Crime."

According to the article, the factory will be shut down for several weeks while the authorities investigate the circumstances and extent of the toxic dumping. There's a quote from Stan Harbishaw professing shock that such things went on in his factory and promising immediate action and the funding of a river cleanup effort.

A GC evaluator should be free of personal vanity, but I read the article over and over, and each time I feel a surge of pride. There is a photo captioned "Hero Student—Tom Filber." The photo was taken outside, and I am smiling so widely that the sunlight glints off my braces.

I told the reporters that I had been inspired to take action by one of my teachers. It's nice to see Arthur Stringfellow mentioned by name in the article, and called a "longtime teacher and environmental activist." I think he would have been proud of that description.

The second article is smaller and lower down: "Experts Confirm Endangered Fish in Town River. Division of Fish and Wildlife to Set Up Immediate Study." There's a file photo of a brown speckled mucker swimming just above a gravel bank.

I walk to school that day with more than the usual trepidation. My brief time as a freshman in high school on Planet Earth has taught me that each time you step outside the norm you are taking your life in your hands. Several of my fellow students at Winthrop P. Muller High School have parents who work at the paint factory, and I suspect they will not be overjoyed at the temporary shutdown.

I use my earth street smarts to dodge and weave my way to school, but once I enter the front door there is no place to hide. Several students glare at me openly, and one girl I don't know walks up and tells me that I should mind my own business. I don't blame her for being angry—I understand she's worried about her parent's job.

I pass Jason Harbishaw in the hall between classes, and he stares at me with smoldering fury. "Didn't I warn you what happens to people who mess with my family?" he demands, his fingers clenching into fists.

"This wasn't about your family," I tell him. "The river belongs to all of us."

"You don't know what you've done," he growls, stepping

toward me as if he intends to exact revenge right away, even though the hall is crowded with students and teachers.

"Here comes Miss Schroeder, our school psychologist," I sing out loudly. "Since you seem so upset, you might want to have a talk with her."

Jason controls himself with an effort. "What goes around, comes around," he whispers and stalks off.

Miss Schroeder beams a big smile in my direction. "I'm so proud of you," she says. Then she surprises me by stepping closer and giving me a congratulatory hug.

Several of my fellow students also surprise me. Sue Ellen walks up to me outside our English class trailer and says, "Hi, Tom. It was so cool of you to give credit to Mr. Stringfellow." It sounds strange to hear one of my classmates call me anything but Alien.

"Thanks," I tell her. "How's your swamp project coming? Are you finding more cats?"

"We found a litter of kittens and I took one home," she says. Then she asks, "Weren't you afraid to go into that big factory all alone at night?"

I notice that Michelle is listening from a few feet away. I give her a quick glance to see if she wants to share the credit. She shakes her head.

"To be honest, I didn't feel like I was alone," I tell Sue Ellen. "It felt like someone who cared about me was helping me every step of the way. Maybe it was Mr. Stringfellow's spirit. Or it could have been my comrades up in the spaceship."

Sue Ellen treats it as a joke and laughs. "I guess it's not so bad to always have little green men watching out for you."

"Yes, it feels very nice not to be completely alone on Planet Earth," I reply. Michelle smiles and gives a tiny nod of agreement, and I see her blue eyes sparkle.

The most surprising conversation of the day occurs in the dreaded locker room as I am about to head out for gym. I change near the door so that if I am attacked I can run out or shout for help. When I see Zitface striding over, I tense up. But instead of threatening me, he waves and says, "Hey, Alien. You've got your shorts on backward."

I glance down. "Thanks."

"I saw your picture in the paper," he continues. "My family has a summerhouse about ten miles downriver. It kinda sucks because we can't swim or fish anymore. Some days the water stinks so bad we can't even wade in." He stops and hesitates for a second. "My father asked me if I knew you. He said to tell you that you've got balls."

I look back at him. "What kind of balls does your dad think I have?"

Zitface appears confounded. "Big ones, I guess."

"I have a basketball that's pretty big," I tell him. "And I have a golf ball that's much smaller."

"Forget it, Alien," he says. "The point is, my dad thinks what you did was pretty amazing." He hesitates, and looks a little embarrassed. "You know, when we kid around with you and roughhouse, we don't mean anything bad by it. You kind of brought it on yourself with all the alien stuff."

I look back at him. "Yes, as you know from reading my letters on the Net, I come from a civilization far more advanced than anything ever seen here on Earth. Our mastery of science is particularly advanced, which has led to great progress in the field of medicine."

Zitface is staring at me as if he regrets coming over. "What are you talking about?"

"Of course, many terrible diseases and plagues still exist in the galaxy," I continue quickly. "For example, there was a recent outbreak of microtic plague on Bubos VII. The good news is that a vast number of health scourges have been completely eradicated by our super sophisticated doctors and scientists."

"I'm not sure where you're going with this, Alien," Zitface says, glancing at the wall clock. "But we'd better get out to gym before Mr. Curtis makes us do penalty sit-ups."

"For example," I tell him in a slightly lower voice, "Confederation scientists have been remarkably successful with skin problems."

Zitface's hands rise to his face self-consciously. He manages to look dubious but intrigued at the same time. "They have?"

"Through a combination of diet and ultra effective cleansing creams, they have stamped out the ravages of acne throughout the known universe."

Zitface blinks back at me. "Look, Alien, we both know there's no spaceship up there . . . But at the same time I . . . How exactly did they stamp it out?"

"Eat less junk food," I suggest softly. "Avoid anything

that's fried or has sugar. Fish, broccoli, and whole grains are good. I might be able to get the spaceship that isn't there to beam down some ultra special cream. Of course, since the spaceship doesn't exist, the cream won't be real either, so if I get it for you, I will not have gotten it for you, and you can't tell anyone. Is that clear?"

Zitface is trying so hard to follow this that his eyes roll around in his head like someone is playing marbles with his pupils. "I think I got it," he says. "Since you're not really an alien, there won't be any miracle cream, even though if it works I'll be really grateful, but I won't tell anyone, because it could never have existed. Right?"

"Spot on," I agree.

He runs out, and I follow him through a short hallway and out a door onto the sunny athletic field. The smell of the grass and the leaves is sweet. For a moment I drink in the beautiful autumn afternoon and remember Miss Schroeder's hug and Sue Ellen's good wishes. It is a strange feeling to be smiling while at school.

Mr. Curtis hurries over and puts an end to my moment of joy. "Filber, stop grinning like an idiot! You think just 'cause you got your picture in the newspaper you can show up late to my class? Drop down and give me twenty stomach crunches! I'd better see you throw a decent spiral soon or you're going to be running penalty laps till your legs fall off!"

The crunches make my stomach burn, and put pressure on other parts of my anatomy. *Get me out of this reeking tunnel,* Tom Filber pleads from my colon.

Sorry, I can't trust you, I tell him.

You can. I've learned my lesson. I'll never advise you to go for tongue action again. You are not just a highly evolved galactic diplomat, but also a major stud here on earth. Now please release me or excrete me. I can't stand this anymore.

I spot Mr. Curtis glaring at me. *I might let you have another chance,* I tell Tom. *But your job is to help me during my mission.*

I'll do my best.

Any advice about throwing a spiral?

Grip it across the laces. Spin it out of your hand.

I try to follow his directions, but the football floats out end over end.

My spiral still sucks.

Don't blame me. I've never been able to throw a decent pass, either.

"Filber," Mr. Curtis barks, "that's a pathetic attempt at a spiral. You look like you have your head up your ass."

"Close," I tell him. "I'm having a discussion with my colon."

"Five penalty laps for having a wise mouth!" he growls. "Start running."

40

When I get home, I see my father's old car parked in the driveway. He is in the kitchen, talking to my mother. I do not mean to eavesdrop, but I find that if I stand near the kitchen door and hold my breath I can almost hear what they're saying.

Crouch down, Tom Filber suggests helpfully. Even though he is still lodged in my colon, I can tell that he is very happy that his father has returned. *Put your ear to the keyhole.*

I take pity on him. *Thanks for the tip.* I suck him back up through my intestine with a reverse flatus, allow him to re-enter the bloodstream, guide him up through the blood-brain barrier, and soon he is once again lodged in the parietal lobe. *Better?* I ask.

You have no idea.

I put my ear to the keyhole and hear my mother say, "Sure, I remember Brad Murcer. He was a punk."

"He's got a carpet-laying business over in Millgate."

"Since when do you know anything about carpet laying?"

"Since he hired me and I just about broke my back for the last three days," my father tells her. "Here, count your money."

She is silent for a few seconds. "Well, this will help, Graham. But Millgate is pretty far away. Driving back and forth will be hard . . ."

"Who said anything about driving back and forth?" he asks. "Brad's renting me a spare room so I have a place to crash four nights a week. I'll come home Fridays and stay through the weekend."

"What kind of husband and father can you be if you're away all week?"

"The kind who helps pay the bills," he tells her sharply. "Take the money. Put some food on the table and get the braces off our son's teeth."

"Okay," she agrees. "We'll do this your way." And then her voice softens. "I'm glad you came home, Graham."

"Did you think I wouldn't?"

"I didn't know."

"Neither did I," he admits. "That first night I just drove and drove. I kept thinking about how we started out so young and in love, and the bitter place we ended up. Ruth, we have to try to make things a little more pleasant around here. Now where is that son of mine?"

I take a few quick steps backward, just in time. He bursts out through the kitchen door and sees me, and his face lights up. "So there's the big hero."

"You read the newspaper?"

"Saw it first thing this morning when I was getting a cup of coffee at the Millgate Diner. I let out a whoop and people looked at me like I was crazy. I told them 'That's my boy. He's striking a blow for his old dad.' "

"I wasn't trying to get revenge for you," I tell him. "I was just trying to protect the river."

"Good," he says. He runs a hand through his hair, which seems to have turned much grayer in just a few days. "Because I've decided I can't go through the rest of my life blaming Stan Harbishaw for everything. Of course, I can blame the bastard for a lot of things. But I dug myself a hole, and I'm the one who has to crawl out of it."

I nod. "Yes, the inability to take responsibility for one's own actions is a prevalent human failing, and at the root of much earthly misery."

His eyes widen. "Where are you from? Mars?"

"Sandoval IV. It's three hundred thousand light-years away."

He stares back at me, and then bursts into a loud laugh. "Oh, sure, that place," he says, finally recovering. "And what do fathers and sons do on Sandoval IV when they want to have a good time and get reacquainted?"

"They roll in the mud and squeak."

"I'm willing to squeak," he says. "I'm not sure about rolling in the mud. Anything else, Tom?"

I look into his kind brown eyes. He is really trying very hard. I sense that over the past few days he has hit rock bottom, and somehow found the strength to go on. The courage of Earthlings to overcome their debacles and try to make a fresh start can be truly heroic. "You came back just in time to teach me something," I tell him. "I need to learn to throw a spiral."

"You mean with a football?"

"Yes. Mr. Curtis, my gym teacher, makes me do crunches and run laps because my spirals aren't tight enough. In fact, they're not really spirals at all."

"Son," he says with a smile, "there are many things about life I can't teach you, but I can show you how to throw the tightest spiral in Barrisford." He looks down and I see that he is still wearing his sweaty carpet-laying clothes and work boots. "There's an old football in the garage," he tells me, "near the bicycle rack. See if you can find it. I'm going to change and I'll meet you out front in ten minutes."

He heads upstairs, and I walk out the door and take a few steps toward the garage. A familiar voice stops me. "Hey, Alien. So this is where you live, huh?"

It's Zitface. He gestures to a blue van parked near the curb. "My dad wants to talk to you." There is a strange look on his face. He appears extremely uncomfortable. Perhaps he is a bit ashamed of how badly he once treated me.

"Your father?" I repeat.

"Yeah," he says. "I think he wants to invite you to our summerhouse."

I veer off toward the blue van. The back door is open. "My father's moving some stuff around," Zitface explains. He calls out, "Hey, Dad! He's here."

A muffled voice calls out from inside the van, "Tom

Filber? Is that you? You're a real hero. Come here for a minute."

I step closer. "No, I'm not a hero . . ." I start to say.

Hands reach out from the back of the van and grab me. I am lifted off my feet and pulled inside by Jason Harbishaw. "Gotcha," he says.

41

I struggle to escape but there are three of them—Jason, Scott, and Zitface. They are too strong for me. They drag me into the van and shut the back door.

I open my mouth to scream, but Jason Harbishaw slugs me in the stomach. He has the size and muscles of a grown man, and the blow knocks the air out of my lungs. He pulls out a piece of rope and quickly ties my arms.

I glance at Zitface and gasp, "Why are you doing this?"

His small black eyes harden. "There's no spaceship," he mutters. "You were making fun of me."

"The problem, Filber, is that you don't know who to trust," Jason tells me, finishing with a knot. "Still," he says, "there's something strange going on. Someone's been helping you." He orders Scott and Zitface, "Find that package of doughnuts he wrote about and get rid of it."

They search me and soon find the stale sugar doughnuts wrapped in tinfoil that contain my wibbler. "We don't need this," Scott says, and flings it out a window.

Jason climbs through to the driver's seat and switches the engine on. "Time for payback, Filber," he growls. "Didn't I warn you that what goes around comes around?"

The van pulls out and heads down the block.

I don't need street smarts to understand that the situation is already dire and growing more dangerous by the second. I make one last desperate attempt to kick open the rear door, but Scott and Zitface grab me.

Through the small window in the back of the van I catch a fleeting look at my father, who has just stepped out of our house. He is dressed in shorts and a T-shirt, and he appears to be whistling. He looks around for me, but I don't believe he sees me as they wrestle me to the floor and the van takes off down Beech Avenue.

We drive very fast. Jason puts on some loud, pounding music with violent lyrics. Someone—I believe it is Shorty D. Long—is rapping about getting even. The chorus seems to be: "What goes around, comes around, I'll bust you up, put you in the ground."

Jason must have taken his new favorite expression from this song.

I access the consciousness of Tom Filber. *What's my next move?*

You don't have a next move, he tells me.

Give me some advice. I'm scared.

I'm petrified, he admits. *Try begging for mercy. And if that doesn't work, pray.*

A Level-Five GC Evaluator should be able to keep a cool head at all times. Nonetheless, I am so afraid that I cannot think clearly. I hear myself begging for mercy but Scott and Zitface just laugh. Sandovinians have not worshipped a divinity for several million years, but I say a few quick prayers anyway.

God does not answer me. The only sound in the van is Shorty D. Long thundering from the speakers: "What gets lost doesn't get found, gonna bust you up, put you in the ground."

I feel dizzy, and I think I may have wet my pants. My wibbler is gone, I have been tied up and punched in the stomach, and my enemies have kidnapped me and now have me completely in their power.

My only hope is that the spaceship is back in Earth's orbit and my comrades are monitoring my progress. But on a protracted mission like this, even top GC crewmen tend to get a bit lazy. They will glance at the screens at regular intervals, but they don't watch me every second. I came to this van of my own free will, and I am riding with kids from school. Even if flight personnel happen to check up on me in the next few minutes, they will conclude that I am taking a trip with some friends. They may not realize my predicament till it is too late.

I should be constructing a plan of escape, but my mind is whirling in other directions. All I can think about is that I foolishly put myself in this position. I should have returned to the spaceship right after Michelle and I got back from the paint factory. I have gained sufficient insight into the human condition to finish my report. My father needs me on Sandoval. And the truth is I had no right to continue to appropriate the body of Tom Filber.

I realize now that I resisted leaving because I wanted to bask in the glory of my triumph at the factory. I wanted to enjoy the newfound respect of my schoolmates. And I especially wanted to spend more time with Michelle Peabody. In my terror, I admit to myself a strange truth: in many ways it is more fun to be a human, living a wacky, unpredictable life on Planet Earth, than to be a GC evaluator cruising the stars. Needless to say, as Jason's van speeds along, I now regret some of my rash choices.

I lift my head a few inches and glimpse trees out the window. We have left the town of Barrisford far behind. I want to ask where we are going and what will become of me, but I am afraid I will be punched again. Earthlings are unpredictable and violent. Anything might happen.

The van pulls off the main road onto a rough path. I feel the tires grind over gravel and bump over rocks. Finally we jerk to a stop.

Jason opens the back door and I see that we are in some thick woods, near the Hoosaguchee River. He grabs me by my left arm and hauls me out. "Any last words, Filber?"

42

face him and attempt to sound calm. "If what goes around comes around, you should be very careful what you do to me," I tell him. "I am protected on Earth by the laws of the United States of America, and in space by an interstellar ship of the Galactic Confederation equipped with technology far beyond your feeble imagination."

He does not look particularly impressed. "You trespassed on my family property and scared my mom. Then you snuck into our factory at night like a little rat. And now our whole operation is going to be shut down because of your meddling. I don't care who's protecting you. You're going to get what's coming to you." He grabs the loose end of the rope that he used to tie my wrists and begins dragging me toward the river.

I dig my heels in to stop him but the bank is sandy and he has a full head of steam. I trip and go down to my knees, and Jason drags me along so quickly that I can't get back to my feet. Stones and sand scrape skin off my legs and arms.

Soon Jason wades out into the cold river and I flounder along a few feet behind him. I swallow mouthfuls of water and cough it back up.

I see Scott and Zitface standing on the bank. Scott is smiling but Zitface looks a little scared. "I think he's had enough, Jace," he says. "You said you were just going to scare him."

"He's got to pay for what he did," Jason growls, stepping closer to me.

Suddenly a loud boom echoes over the treetops. It could be the sound of a plane breaking the sound barrier, or of an interstellar spaceship swooping overhead. For a second the tree branches rustle and bow down, and even Jason looks a bit spooked.

"What the hell was that?" Scott asks.

"Just a plane or maybe a helicopter," Jason says, trying to sound matter-of-fact, but I hear doubt in his voice. "They take off from Fairfield Airport and like to buzz these woods sometimes." The three of them crane their necks, searching for the plane.

I take advantage of the distraction to try to escape. A rock offers my feet some traction. I lunge away from Jason, and at the same time yank the rope with all my strength. He keeps hold of it and staggers. For a moment we're both off balance. I kick out with my legs, and my foot connects with his ankle. He falls into the Hoosaguchee face-first.

I stagger away, but he's on me in a second. He grabs me by the hair and yanks so hard it feels like my scalp may come off. I scream.

"This is what happens to people who mess with the Harbishaws," he snarls. He puts his big right hand on the crown of my skull like he's palming a basketball and forces me under the surface.

I hold my breath and fight back with every ounce of strength that I have, but I can't break his grip. My mouth finally opens, and river water pours in. I feel myself start to black out. Consciousness dwindles to a rope, then frays to a single thread, and that thread stretches taut.

So this is what it feels like to drown. It is not a pleasant way to die. It is slow and agonizing. I hear Tom Filber bellowing in pain and fear from the Ragwellian Bubble. He is not giving me advice or even speaking words. He is just making a terrible, scared, pitiful wail.

The realization that I am about to die gives me one last desperate surge of energy. I push off the bottom of the river with my palms and force my head up, and somehow I find the strength to shake Jason's grip. I explode above the surface and try to suck in a breath, but it feels like I have swallowed half the river. All I can do is puke and retch and try to stumble away.

"Where do you think you're going?" Jason demands.

And then my dad's voice rumbles from very close, "If you touch him again, Jason Harbishaw, I promise you'll regret it for the rest of your life."

43

I see and hear everything that happens next in fragmented bits and pieces as I try to recover from nearly being drowned.

Jason Harbishaw forgets all about me. He yells, "I don't let old washed-up drunks tell me what to do," and charges toward my father.

My father is a blur as he runs into the river toward Jason.

Out of the corner of my eye I register that someone else is crashing through the bushes toward the riverbank, issuing loud orders for everyone to stand still.

I am fixated on the collision that is about to take place, and I fear the result. Jason is only eighteen, but he must weigh more than two hundred pounds and he's a broad-shouldered bull of a teenager. My father is tall and gaunt and more than two decades older. I'm afraid that Jason will run right over him.

As they get close, Jason draws back his right fist and

throws a whistling roundhouse punch that tears my father's head off. Or at least it would decapitate my dad if the blow connected. But my father ducks under the sweeping punch, lowering his center of gravity at the last second.

There's the smacking sound of a bone-jarring collision, and I hear Jason cry out in surprise and pain as he flies backward and disappears into the river. It occurs to me that my father was once a defensive end on an undefeated state champion football team, and he can still hit pretty hard.

My father turns to me. His expressive eyes are filled with concern. "Are you okay?"

"I swallowed a lot of water, but . . . WATCH OUT, DAD!" I shout.

Jason has surfaced, and something dark and heavy gleams in his hand. It's a sharp-edged rock he's pulled off the river bottom. He tries to bash my father's head in with it, but Dad ducks out of the way at the last second.

"DROP THE ROCK," a voice commands from the bank. "WALK OUT OF THE RIVER WITH YOUR HANDS WHERE I CAN SEE THEM."

I look over and see Sergeant Collins standing on the bank with his gun drawn.

Jason glances at him, and then back at my father. His baby face curls up with a look of all-consuming rage. "DAMN YOU," he growls. Instead of dropping the rock, he steps toward my dad again, drawing back his arm for another swipe.

A gunshot rings out. I have never heard one before. It is a piercing whine, a shocking and unmistakable sound. I believe Sergeant Collins has just fired a warning shot over Jason's head.

"This is your last warning," the policeman shouts. "Drop the rock and walk out now!"

The shot gets even Jason Harbishaw's attention. His big right hand opens and the glittering black rock splashes back into the Hoosaguchee. He slowly raises his hands and starts walking toward the bank.

"Did he hurt you?" my father asks.

"No," I tell him. "You came just in time."

Meanwhile, Jason has reached the bank. He begins to mutter something about my father attacking him, and says that Scott and Zitface will back up his story.

But the two younger boys look scared and keep silent, and Sergeant Collins cuts in and says he saw the whole thing. He tells Jason to lie flat on the bank, and begins to handcuff his hands behind his back. "You're under arrest for suspicion of kidnapping, attempted murder, assault with a deadly weapon, and a whole lot of other things we can get into later," he says. "You have the right to remain silent . . . "

I don't hear the rest because my father puts his arms around me. "Thank God I found you," he says. "I followed the van and called the police. But when he turned off the highway I lost you for a second . . ."

I hug him back. "We're both okay. That's the important thing."

"You're right," he agrees, and I feel his body shiver as he hugs me even more tightly. He is trembling now. I remind myself that he's been through a lot in the past few days. "We're going to be okay from now on," he whispers. "We're going to be just fine."

We stay like that for a minute or two, holding on to each other, knee-deep in the river. Finally I tell him, "Dad, I think it's time to go home."

44

The stars are bright in the cloudless night sky, blazing like fiery beacons that summon me homeward.

"So what's your final conclusion about Planet Earth and species Homo sapiens?" Michelle Peabody whispers.

We are sitting in her swing, beneath a blanket because the autumn night has a chilly bite to it. We have just spent more than two hours doing absolutely nothing except cuddling and talking and listening to the crickets. It is nearly time for her to go into her house, and I am contemplating a homeward journey of my own. The thought makes me happy, but also fills me with regret.

"I think humans are the most misunderstood species in the known universe," I tell her. "Observed from a far vantage point, they manifest cruel, illogical, and self-destructive behavior. But when one actually inhabits a sensitive and vulnerable human body—especially a fourteen-year-old body—and has to deal with all of the unpredictable, crazy, heartbreaking, gut-wrenching things that can happen to you on Planet Earth—most humans are doing the best that they can. And some of them are among the nicest organisms I have met in all my travels through this vast galaxy."

She tilts her head thoughtfully and then smiles and kisses me softly on the lips. "I've never been called an organism before."

"Do you like it?"

"Not particularly."

I trace my hand through the tiny blond curls near her ears. I bend close and inhale her—the fragrance of her hair, of her clothes, of her body. I run my finger along the rim of her lips, and she nips me with her teeth and giggles. "I'm going to miss you terribly," I tell her.

"You'll always know where to find me," she says. "I'm just the earth girl next door, 332 Beech Avenue, Terra Firma. Come and see me whenever you get the space blues. Or stay here a little longer. There's lots more that needs to be evaluated." Her hand finds mine under the blanket, and our fingers intertwine.

"You don't really believe anything I've told you about my mission, do you?" I whisper.

She looks back into my eyes. "I believe you've been through something difficult and unusual. You've grown and changed a lot. And I'm so glad you're okay. I keep thinking of those boys grabbing you. If your father hadn't come . . ." She stops whispering and a tear squeezes out of her blue eye and runs down her cheek.

I wipe it away. "It's getting late," I tell her. "We should probably both be heading home."

She nods and stands. "Bye, Alien. I think I'm falling in love with you a little bit."

I stand also, and give her a farewell embrace. GC evaluators are supposed to have tight control over their emotions, but I am blinking away tears of my own. "Bye, earth girl next door," I whisper back. "You may have redeemed your entire species."

She grins. "You're just a snail who's a sucker for a blonde."

"Can I help it?" I ask her. "You're a very special organism."

She leans in, so that our lips are almost touching. "How special?" she whispers.

"Exceedingly special," I whisper back.

"I'll take that," she murmurs. She glances at her watch. "Gotta go. School tomorrow. Bye."

She kisses me one last time, then hops off the swing and walks away quickly, toward her house.

I watch her fade into the darkness. I listen to her light footsteps walking across her porch. The screen door shuts and she is gone.

I tilt my head back and look up at the Milky Way. There are roughly one hundred billion stars in the galaxy, many of them larger and brighter than the Earth's sun. Orbiting those stars are an even greater number of planets, with far more interesting geological and aquatic features than can be found anywhere on Earth. And populating those planets are a nearly infinite number of life-forms. In the Galactic Confederation we list more than ten thousand member species, all of them more peaceful and intelligent than human beings.

But none of that matters to me right now. I sit in the swing and look up at the shadowy outline of Michelle's house, and suck in a deep breath of cold autumn air.

Finally I rise and cross the hedge barrier to the Filber backyard. This was my point of entry, and this is where they are waiting for me to give the signal. I stand beneath the crab apple tree, looking up at the house.

It is a small and dilapidated structure, but it has gotten to feel like home. Dissonant cello music is coming from Sally's room. There is an Earth saying that absence makes the heart grow fonder, but even when I'm a million light-years away, I doubt I'll miss my sister.

From Sally's room, my eyes rise to the attic office. The light is off up there, and the TV is off, too.

Instead, I see a light glowing from my parents' bedroom. They are there together, and I believe they are at peace.

I raise my arms skyward and rotate my palms in a Locurian Estevel Pattern—GC sign language for "I'm ready to go." I feel the first tug of the reverse gravity beam. It lifts me a few inches off the lawn and then it sets me gently back down on the grass.

Why did it stop? Oh, yes. I forgot. There is one last thing I need to do.

Tom, are you ready?

Ready and waiting, he answers eagerly.

Thank you for your body, I tell him. *I have enjoyed it.*

You're welcome, I guess, he replies. *Come back and visit sometime. But please stay out of my nostrils and cranium.*

Fair enough, I agree. *And you try to limit your intake of potato chips. As far as throwing a spiral goes, I believe the trick is in turning the wrist.*

Will this hurt? he asks.

Not a bit, I assure him. *But there will be a few moments of disorientation. Just stay calm and relaxed. You're going back to a very familiar place.*

I concentrate my energies, suction Tom Filber's consciousness from the Ragwellian Bubble, and relocate it in its original spot inside his cerebrum. As he enters, I leave, using a reverse Thromborg to detach myself. I exit through the right nasal passage. It's dark and slimy so I don't waste time. Right turn, left turn, crawl around, slither over, and I pop out into the cool night air.

As soon as I am exposed, the reverse gravity beam lifts me into the air. I am drawn upward at great speed and soon see the shadowy outline of our spaceship hovering above me.

I am pulled in through the cargo bay doors, and in a few seconds I am back in my protective shell, accepting the congratulations of the Preceptor and all my old friends. "The Council of Elders has sent you a special citation for surviving the barbarities of Planet Earth alone, when we were called to Bubos VII," he says proudly.

"Those humans were vicious. Hideous!" a Rygenian engineer says, shaking her four heads sympathetically.

"Yes, they can be brutal," I agree. And then I add softly, "But they do have their redeeming qualities."

"Good news about your father," the Preceptor says. "He's out of danger and back in the Ketchvar burrow."

"Thank you, that is good news," I say. "I can't wait to see him."

"Well, you'll see him soon enough," the Preceptor assures me. "We might as well pull out of orbit and head for Sandoval."

"Sounds like a plan," I agree. And then I ask, "If you don't mind, could I just watch on the screens what's happening at 330 Beech Avenue? I just want to make sure Tom Filber is okay. We owe him that much."

The Preceptor nods to the technician on duty, and a second later the Filbers' backyard comes on the main screen. Tom Filber is standing right beneath the crab apple tree, blinking. This is normal recuperative behavior for someone who has just been released from a Ragwellian Bubble.

"He looks fine," the Preceptor says. "By the way, the Confederation would appreciate a preliminary indication of how you intend to conclude your evaluation."

Tom Filber stops blinking and gazes skyward. Then he shrugs and starts walking toward his house. He hears something and stops. Instead of going home, he walks toward the hedge.

"Let's keep watching just a minute more," I tell the Preceptor.

On the screen, I see Tom Filber cross through the hedge into Michelle Peabody's backyard. She has just climbed onto her swing. "Oh, hi, Tom," she says. "I thought you'd gone in. I forgot the blanket and it may rain."

She picks up the blanket and steps off the swing.

Tom Filber walks closer to her and clears his throat. "Michelle," he says hesitantly.

"Yes."

"I'm sorry."

"Sorry for what?" she asks.

He doesn't answer right away. "For being such a jerk," he finally mumbles.

"What are you talking about?" She looks at him more closely, as if she's starting to vaguely sense something.

"I just mean, for living next to you for so many years and not appreciating you," he says. "I would like to get to know you better. We should take things slowly. Is that okay?"

She studies his face in the moonlight and then takes his hand. "Very okay," she whispers, and kisses him almost shyly on the cheek. "Now I'd really better go in."

I turn away from the screen, to the Preceptor. "You can advise the Council of Elders that the Lugonians will not be happy with my decision."

"Indeed?" he responds, sounding surprised. "You believe there is hope for this benighted species?"

"Given a little more time, I think they will surprise us," I answer, watching Tom Filber walk back through the hedge toward his house. He is smiling, and he touches his cheek where Michelle kissed him.

"Now you can take us out of orbit," I tell the navigator. "My mission to Planet Earth is finished."